Praise for
An Intent to Commit

"The First Amendment remains front and center in this legal thriller...The cast is comprised of an eclectic group of complex characters with intriguing backstories. And Lambek, a Vermont attorney, is a meticulous writer who stages even relatively minor scenes with the same descriptive precision he uses in his legal arguments. An engrossing, thoughtful, and disturbing drama that caters to fans of constitutional debates."

—KIRKUS REVIEWS

"Looking for a civil rights whodunit? This book has it all–intrigue, tutorials, politics, good guys, bad guys–all set in Vermont among Vermont lawyers and people who matter. This novel weaves the story of Black Lives Matter versus Second Amendment worshipers as the participants lived it in court, at home and with friends over a cup of coffee. A flag and, yes, a kidnapping, run through it. This tale is at heart an owner's manual on the ABCs of winning a civil rights struggle. It should be required reading in the first year of law school."
—JAMES MORSE, retired Vermont Supreme Court Justice

"Vermont attorney Bernie Lambek, in his second novel, again tells a story about lawyers involved in a controversial case, this time involving civil liberties issues in the current historical moment—the social and political divisions provoked and nurtured by a president, the Black Lives Matter movement, supporters of Second Amendment gun rights, free speech and the First Amendment. The reader of

Lambek's previous novel *Uncivil Liberties* will meet again characters from that story with new personal and legal issues, but need not have read the first novel to enjoy and learn from this one. *An Intent to Commit* is an engaging, thoughtful, and well-written novel."

—STEPHEN WIZNER, William O. Douglas Clinical
Professor Emeritus, Yale Law School

An Intent to Commit

An Intent to Commit

A Novel

Bernie Lambek

Rootstock Publishing

Montpelier, VT

AN INTENT TO COMMIT
Copyright © 2021 by Bernie Lambek
All Rights Reserved.

First Printing: November 16, 2021

Paperback ISBN: 978-1-57869-070-1
Hardcover ISBN: 978-1-57869-073-2
eBook ISBN: 978-1-57869-070-1
Library of Congress Control Number (LCCN): 2021911159

Published by Rootstock Publishing, an imprint of Multicultural Media, Inc.
27 Main Street, Suite 6
Montpelier, VT 05602 USA
www.rootstockpublishing.com
info@rootstockpublishing.com

Email the author at: blambek@zclpc.com

Book design by D. Hoffman
Cover Art (Image) by Susan Bull Riley

Printed in the USA

Author's Note
and Acknowledgments

This is a work of fiction. While many of the places and a few of the events described in the novel are real or close to it, the plot and characters are fictional. Accounts of certain Black Lives Matter events at Montpelier High School, U-32 Middle High School, and the Unitarian Church in Montpelier are largely drawn from the excellent reporting by Stephen Mills and David Delcore in the *Barre Montpelier Times Argus*, specifically articles appearing on August 12, 2015, January 23, 2018, January 29, 2018, February 1, 2018, and June 5, 2018. I have great admiration for the student activists, including Maryann Songhurst, Joelyn Mensa, Mandy Abu Aziz, Latitia Montgomery, Devante Lee, and Mia Smith—some of whose remarks, quoted in the *Times Argus*, I have inserted into my fictional account.

I am grateful to my friend whose writings I harvested to create the emails and texts written by the fictional Tyrene Jean-Pierre in this novel.

This book was mostly written before the pandemic, on the computer in my law office. My partners—Patty Turley, John Page, and Steve Cusick—thought I was doing legal work for clients. Or maybe they knew better. Anyway, I thank them for their indulgence and their camaraderie.

Howard Norman, whose beautiful novels I so admire, read at least two versions of the manuscript and offered his invaluable critique. Jim Morse, a retired justice of the Vermont Supreme Court, read an early draft and graciously gave me honest and sound feedback. My son, Will Lambek, read it too and shared his perceptive insights based on years as an organizer at Migrant Justice Vermont. My friend and fellow lawyer, Denise Bailey, also lent me her discerning perspective on the manuscript. Linda Sproul, my wife, challenged me on the parts that didn't make enough sense. I owe gratitude to all of them, and still more to my editor at Rootstock, Rickey Gard Diamond, for her deep understanding as a writer, and to publisher Stephen McArthur and the magnanimous team at Rootstock.

I apologize to my old friend, Ron Chabot, who once built and lived in a geodesic dome on Poor Farm Road in Thetford Center, Vermont, and who, aside from that fact, could not be more different from the character in this book who chose to live in a similar dome in the same location.

For my sweetheart, Linda

And in memory of
Laurie LeClair
1961-2019

"True threats encompass those statements where the speaker means to communicate a serious expression of an intent to commit an act of unlawful violence to a particular individual or group of individuals."

Virginia v. Black, 123 S.Ct. 1536 (2003)

Contents

Part I: Movement 1

Part II: Patriots 57

Part III: Damages 107

Part IV: The Wrong Place in Life 155

Part I

Movement

Sarah Jacobson turns off the highway at the Randolph exit and pulls into the gas station located next to the exit ramp. As she drives up alongside one of the pumps, she notices that the gray van that came off the ramp right behind her is now stopped in the shadows to the side of the convenience store, behind a couple of tow trucks and pallets stacked with bags of mulch or manure. She looks curiously at the van because it had followed her so closely as she drove off the ramp toward the gas station. About to get out to pump gas, she wonders what the van is doing.

It is a Thursday afternoon in April of 2019, and still cold out. She turns to reach for her coat in the back seat, grabs it and faces forward again, and notices that a large man in a red plaid jacket and a cap pulled low over his face has stepped out of the van and is walking toward her car. She puts her arms through the coat sleeves, and watches the man approaching the pumps.

He is muscle-bound, she can tell, his right arm hanging away from his torso, his legs apart as he walks, his left arm held up to his hat and covering most of his face. He wears dark glasses. Suddenly she is frightened and utterly unsure of what is coming next and how she should handle it, whatever it is.

She thinks: Should I drive away and get out of here?

She thinks: Do I have anything that could be used as a weapon?

She thinks: That's ridiculous. I don't know this guy. Why am I being paranoid?

Sarah is not a person easily afraid. But now she is afraid.

The man, his gloved hand held over his face, yanks open the rear door and heaves himself into her car.

Even before she can speak, the intruder instructs, "Don't look at me. Start your car and drive." The fear now rises up Sarah's spine into her throat. "Start your car and drive," he repeats, soft and calm. "I've got a gun."

Sarah turns on the engine.

"Drive to the park-and-ride on the other side of the highway," the intruder tells her. The parking lot, used by commuters and ride-sharers, is just a couple of hundred yards away. Sarah does what she is told to do, not having the wits even to contemplate alternatives.

"Here," he says, indicating a space in the park-and-ride lot. Sarah parks. She looks around the lot and sees no one. He gets out of her car and says through the open door, "Now you get out slowly. Keep your eyes down."

The man comes around to her front door, again with one arm covering his face. As she steps out, she sees the gun in his hand. She wonders fleetingly whether he could use it with gloves on.

"Lock the car. Give me the keys. Look down." She does these things.

"Give me your phone." It's in her back pocket and she gives it to him. "We are going to walk back to my van, like we're friends. I'll take your arm, like this, and be a step behind you. Got it?" He doesn't wait for an answer and pushes her forward. He smells like woodsmoke and creosote.

In her mind she is now running through options. Scream? Run? Play nice? Find out what he wants? Offer something? She feels his strong hand gripping her arm tightly. She tries the fourth option. "What is it you want, sir?"

He doesn't answer, but he keeps his hand around her arm from behind and pushes her along. He said they would walk like they're friends. She thinks how absurd that is.

There was a moment when she was getting out of the car when she glimpsed part of the man's face and she tries to imagine it again as he is marching her back to the gas station. She thinks that maybe the face is familiar, but she isn't sure.

"What do you want?" Sarah asks again.

"I want you to shut up," he answers.

The man marches her this way to his van, Sarah afraid and compliant. He opens the side door and makes her get inside. There is some kind of a harness already set up in the seat and he puts it around her, with a strap going around her arms that he cinches and clamps somehow behind the seat, and she is unable to move her arms or get out of the seat.

"I can't move," she gasps, for no reason. She imagines how Ricky will feel when he learns she is gone or dead. Her fear is accompanied by immeasurable sadness.

The man now puts a paper bag over her head and places a rubber band around the paper bag, at the level of her chin. She cannot see anything, and it is hard to breathe. Sarah feels tears in her eyes. The van motor coughs on and they drive away.

Almost four years earlier, in the middle of August 2015, Sam Jacobson, at home in Montpelier, Vermont, had called his daughter Sarah, then living in Providence, Rhode Island.

"You eating dinner or anything?" he began without introduction.

"Hey, Dad. No, this is a good time. It's only just after five. How're things?"

"I just read this article in today's *Times Argus* and I thought you'd be interested. Do you have a moment?"

"Sure. Do you want to just email it to me?"

"That's too complicated." A typical complaint of his, but she was more tolerant of his technical feebleness than she used to be. "I'm sitting here with the newspaper in my lap. Let me just read it to you. I want you to hear this."

"Okay, Pops. Let me turn off the TV here. Hold on." Sarah did that and also grabbed a beer from the fridge and opened it. "Okay, I'm back."

"How's Ricky?" he now asked.

"Ricky's good. He's at work at the restaurant." He was a line cook and dishwasher at an Italian restaurant.

"Oh, he's still doing that?"

"Yes, he's still doing that," she answered, sounding annoyed at her father being judgmental. "You mentioned an article?"

"Yes, the article. I'll read. 'Calls for greater dialogue on race and violence were expressed at a Sunday evening vigil in Montpelier on the first anniversary of the death of Michael Brown in Ferguson, Missouri.'"

Sarah interrupted. "Did you go?" She sipped the beer. "To the vigil?"

"Yes, yes, we went, Mom and I. I'll tell you in a moment. I want to read you this first. 'Brown, an eighteen-year-old African American, was unarmed when he died August 9, 2014, after being shot by white police officer Darren Wilson. His death sparked widespread protests in Ferguson and across the nation and fueled a growing national conversation about other incidents of African Americans being killed by police officers.' Okay, you know all that. But here's the part about Montpelier: 'About thirty people gathered outside the Unitarian Church on Main Street Sunday to support the national day of mourning for Brown. They held signs that read *Black Lives Matter*, a national rallying cry sparked by Brown's death. Participants also sang songs and observed four and a half minutes of silence to commemorate the four and a half hours Brown lay in the street after his slaying. They were welcomed by the minister of the Unitarian Church.' You've met her?"

"The minister? No. Didn't she recently start in that position?"

"Yeah, I guess you're right. You've been gone a few years, Sarahkins! I forget how long sometimes. We like her, the new minister. Well, it goes on from there a bit. The reporter quotes the reverend saying: 'We have gathered here to support the Black Lives Movement and the lives that have been lost due to racism.' Then it says she distributed a list of names of other African Americans killed by police or who died in police custody."

A list of names. Sarah tensed, and there was silence on the line. But she recognized her father's gesture, his generosity. "You trying to get me to come back to Vermont?"

"No," he lied. "I just want you to know that even here in Montpelier we're moved, we're affected by the Black Lives Matter movement. People are fed up. Even here," he repeated.

"Good," she said. "You said you and Mom went to the vigil?"

"We did. Very powerful. Wish you'd been at our side."

"Me too."

"You would have liked it. It made me think of you, for sure."

She didn't answer and there was another quiet pause on the line.

"I know how much this affects you, Sarah," said her father at last.

He wanted her to know he understood this about her, how the killing of Black men triggered her personal grief. When she was in college—well before she and Ricky were together—she had a boyfriend, Tyrene Jean-Pierre. In January of 2015, Tyrene had been shot and killed by a white cop in New Haven, Connecticut. There was no video of the event and the circumstances had been murky.

The internal police investigation found the killing to have been justified, that the officer who fired bullets into Tyrene had been in reasonable fear that Tyrene posed a threat to the officer's safety. They said Tyrene had a knife and was making threatening moves at the officer. Sarah didn't think Tyrene carried a knife. What she knew was he had black skin.

What she also knew was that he could be, and maybe was at the time of the shooting, irrational and provocative.

"Yes, Dad, it does affect me. It hurts. It was thoughtful of you to call. And for you to tell me you know that."

"I'm so sorry," he said.

"I know."

"*Do* you think about moving back up here?" he asked.

"I'm not planning ahead, but who knows?"

At 7:00 p.m. on a June evening in 2018, Ricky Stillwell showed up for the meeting, nine people in a living room on Sherman Street in Montpelier, Vermont. Most of the people were chatting as they gathered, but Ricky was quiet and listened and waited. The host, Eleanor, who had been eagerly offering her greetings to everyone, now spoke to the group.

"Thank you all for coming tonight!" She was an older woman, Ricky guessed about 75, who smiled broadly as she talked and looked around the room to catch each person's eye.

"You all right? Here, come in and join the circle."

People adjusted their positions, trying to make the circle rounder. Ricky felt he was too close to the woman next to him, and he slid his chair a bit to the left to equalize the distance, trying to keep his long legs and big feet from invading others' spaces.

Ricky looked around the room. Four women, two other men, and two people whose gender he was unsure about. Ricky was twenty-six and felt himself to be the youngest person in the room, but it was hard to judge age. They were all white, or they all appeared to Ricky to be white. He was not always sure about that either.

Eleanor continued: "Okay, welcome! My name is Eleanor. Thank you so much for coming. This is a SURJ conversation meeting. SURJ is Showing Up for Racial Justice. Some folks call it Standing Up for Racial Justice. Or Speaking Up. Show up, speak up, or stand up—it doesn't matter! I hope that's why you're here." Huge smile.

Ricky admired the lines around her eyes, what people sometimes call crow's feet. He thought she looked wise. She had splendid white hair.

"Good, that's good," she said, since no one got up to leave. "We're in a safe space," Eleanor assured the group.

Ricky knew the expression. He thought it meant they should not hurt or criticize one another, but as he pondered that he was not certain. He didn't ask.

"What we want to do is to have honest conversations about race," Eleanor went on. "We are here to be open and to share our perspectives. Is it all right if I spend just a moment outlining the core principles for this meeting?"

It was all right for Ricky, and apparently for everyone, as people nodded their assent. Who could possibly object?

"First core principle: We will listen to each other without judging each other. In this room, no opinion is offered in bad faith. Right? Very important. Second: What we say here is confidential. Meaning, afterwards, we don't talk about who said what. Okay?"

Ricky nodded in agreement. This woman was wonderfully concise. He would like to be more like that. "Third core principle: Be comfortable being uncomfortable."

Whatever this paradox meant, Ricky liked it, and uncomfortable he was.

He had been participating in meetings about racial justice for a few months now, since he and Sarah had moved back to Montpelier. Most of these events were sponsored by the Unitarian Church, his church now. The Unitarian Church, in spite of its name, celebrated diversity. It aspired to be totally inclusive, welcoming believers of all beliefs on matters of religion and non-religion.

Ricky was skeptical about the church's profession of inclusivity because he doubted that true religious conservatives and evangelicals—like the members of the Fellowship Church of the Crucified Savior, the born-again church he had attended during his high school years—would feel welcome at the Unitarian Church. He thought—and he had said this to Sarah when he tried to persuade her, atheist Jew that she was, to attend Unitarian services on Sunday mornings—that the word *church* was a bit of a misnomer.

True, it looked exactly like a church is supposed to look. It had a steeple rising above its immense front doors. And it had rituals a church has. The participants called themselves a *congregation* and they came together on Sunday mornings. A minister delivered a sermon most weeks. They sang. They had moments of quiet or prayer. In form it was a church. But in substance it was less church-like.

The rituals and the sermon and the devotion did not require underlying faith or belief in God or divinity. He called it a faith-neutral environment. It was also a social justice organization and community gathering place. It held regular events and discussions on the subjects of race, gender conformity, inequality, immigration, and related topics. It was one of his fellow Unitarians who told him about the SURJ conversations and introduced him to Eleanor, also a church regular, who had then invited Ricky to come to the meeting on Sherman Street. Sarah wholeheartedly encouraged him to attend.

Ricky missed some of what Eleanor had just said. His mind had wandered off-topic, as it did in every lecture he'd ever attended. He might have missed some core principles! He was sure there were more than three. His focus was drawn back to Eleanor, because she had paused after saying, "I have my own implicit biases. My assumption is each of you do, too. Am I right?"

No one replied, because it would have been impolitic to contest that we harbor implicit biases.

Eleanor was fluent with the vernacular of the movement: implicit bias, white privilege, microaggressions, and so on. The words were useful and important, Ricky thought, but he wondered if they were over-used, like too many sweet delicacies in the diet. Correct words could not, by themselves, substitute for critical thinking. Ricky remembered Sarah's father, Sam, once teasing Sarah when she used the term *lived experience*.

No need to be redundant, he had grumbled at her. She got angry with him. He deflected by joking that he would get a court order to cease and desist using redundancies. She remained irritated. Come on, Sarah, he said, I'm making fun of myself here, making fun of lawyers and how they talk. Ah, said Sarah, okay, I get it, very funny.

Now Eleanor said, "We in this room, here in this sheltering Vermont room, must acknowledge our privilege, and that is a starting place." She smiled directly at Ricky and Ricky, not smiling, nodded his acknowledgment. "Any questions before we move on?" No questions, some shuffling of bottoms on chairs. Some sniffles.

"What I want to suggest to begin," Eleanor went on, with Ricky trying to keep focus, "is instead of introducing ourselves to the group right off, we talk to the person next to us. Except it's best if it's a person you don't know well. So, if you're sitting next to your best friend or your mother," the big smile again, "find someone else to pair up with. Learn something about that person, and you will each introduce that person when we come back to the full meeting. Hmm?"

Ricky glanced to his left and his right.

"And just take a few minutes, let's say no more than five minutes." Eleanor looked around the circle again with her teacher's smile. "But there's a bit more to this. It's not hard! I'm going to give you one task, one theme, all right? Each of you share with your neighbor an experience you have had where you were *uncomfortable*"—this seemed to be Eleanor's favored word—"because of some incident in your personal lives relating to *race* or *bigotry*, and how you dealt with it. For example, did you *confront* the situation, or did you let it go by, and how did it make you *feel*?"

Ricky noticed her up-and-down speech, her emphasis on certain words. In his attention to her intonation, he again lost the thread of the content. "That sort of thing." What sort of thing? he wondered.

"Could be almost anything, you see. Does everyone understand?" People nodded once more and murmured. "You know, five minutes is just not realistic," said Eleanor. "Let's make it ten minutes."

Ricky looked around at his compatriots, who all seemed to know what they were doing. The group did a dance so that everyone paired up and moved around so they could have one-on-one conversations. Ricky found himself next to a man in the front corner of the room, by the woodstove.

"I'm Joe," said this guy, and Ricky said, "Hi, my name's Ricky Stillwell. I'm not really sure, maybe you go first?"

Joe was thirty-something with a shaved head, and he leaned forward eagerly. "You want me to? Okay. I live in Barre, grew up in Williamstown. I've never been to one of these before. So, yeah, I have a story about race. I was at this gym I go to in Burlington, where I used to live for a while, called Jump 'n Pump. I was working out on one of those stair machines and this guy on the machine next to me starts talking to me. His head is shaved, like mine, so I guess he relates to me. He has a great big beard, but his head's like a cue ball."

Ricky admired and envied Joe's ability to spin out sentences. Joe didn't slow down. "We talked about a bunch of things, I don't know. This guy's a lawyer, he says. He works for a firm in Burlington. That kinda surprised me a bit, just based on his looks." Joe stopped for a second. "Ha. I suppose that's my implicit bias."

Ricky smiled at Joe, unsure.

"You know, like judging from his looks he wouldn't be a lawyer. I remember," Joe continued, "we talked for a while about cars. He was into muscle cars, you know what I'm talking about? And I kinda used to be a motorhead. I had a Mustang a few years ago. We talked about that. Then—here's the thing—the guy says he just came back from Charlottesville. This was right after Charlottesville, you know, the place in Virginia where the Nazis or Neo-Nazis or whatever marched around, and that woman was killed when some guy plowed his car into the crowd of people who were there to tell the fucking Nazis to go home."

Ricky swallowed, let his jaw drop, and he nodded for Joe to keep going.

"He was *there* in Charlottesville. Well, I'm just keeping on working out on my StairMaster, and the guy says, *Fucking immigrants.*

Fucking Jewish Communists! It must be my shaved head or something that he thinks I'm like sympathetic with him. I couldn't believe it. I didn't know what to say and I really didn't want to look at him. Maybe I said, *oh, yeah*, or something lame like that, but mostly I was quiet and then I got off the machine and told the guy I was done with my workout. I told him I had to be somewhere, you know?

"I tried not to be rude. He grinned at me and said something like, *Nice talking with you, man.* That was it. I didn't confront him. I didn't know how. I even said it was good talking with him too. The whole thing made me feel pretty bad. I'm sure not proud of it."

Joe looked intently at Ricky for a moment, and Ricky wondered if he saw tears brimming at the edges of his eyes. "Those words, *Jewish Communists*, all that stuff, really stuck in my head," Joe finally said.

Ricky sat silently, unsure of himself, smitten by Joe's story.

"What about you?" Joe asked him. "Sorry, tell me your name again. I was kinda focused on my story, and I forgot your name."

"Ricky," said Ricky. "That's okay. This dude was a lawyer, for real?"

"That's what he said."

"I'm trying to figure out how I would have reacted," Ricky said. Ricky was a person who usually spoke his mind, once he'd made up his mind, unafraid of the consequences. This trait had gotten him into trouble in the past, to put it mildly. And that's what now came into his mind.

"Okay. I live in Montpelier now, and I grew up here too," Ricky said. "But I spent the last couple of years in Rhode Island, in Providence. I was in college in New York before that." He paused and took a deep breath. "My story goes like this— It's not about race *per se*," he told Joe, "but it is about bigotry. I'll put it that way. Do you think that fits enough with this theme here?"

"Sure, go ahead," said Joe.

"I used to be in a church, as a teenager, years ago, and I was really anti-gay. I mean I was taught that homosexuality went against the Bible. And I believed that. Not that I feel that way any-more," he wanted Joe to know. "I had a friend in high school who was a lesbian. At one point I told her she was sinning against God and I told her I thought she should be outed at school, you know, like to shame her out of the closet or something. A little later she died in an accident. It was the most terrible thing in my life."

"Oh my god, you're that guy?" said Joe. "I think I read about it."

Eleanor called out to the whole group, "Okay, everyone, let's wrap up and come back into a circle, and you each will have the opportunity to tell the group about your partner's lived experiences."

In her sightless, immobile state, Sarah is paying attention to the feel of the drive. She surmises they are on the interstate but can only guess at direction. At one point in the journey, Sarah asks, "Where are we going?" There is no reply.

Time passes, maybe a half hour? Then there is deceleration and turns right and left, and acceleration and hills as she is pulled this way and that way against the harness that holds her. She is cold. Her eyes are closed and she tries to breathe calmly. Friends have instructed her on the importance of deep breaths, and she tries to recall what she should do with her breathing.

Later she can tell they're on a gravel road. The song "Car Wheels on a Gravel Road" by Lucinda Williams comes to her mind. Her parents often played Lucinda Williams's CDs, and she recalls how they sang that song, growled it is more like it, as they washed dishes together. Her parents! Donna and Sam! How will they deal with this thing that is happening to her? It is her father she sud-denly worries about more than her mother: this will kill him.

The van comes to a stop. She hears the man open his door, get out, slam his door, walk on the gravel, open her door. She is taken out of the harness, not too roughly, and led out of the van, stum-bling, with the paper bag still held around her face. It feels like dirt and rocks underfoot now. She is trying to be careful, taking short steps, trying not to fall, as the man's big hand holds her arm.

He says, "Watch for the step here. And another one." He maneuvers her into a building, where the air is still and quiet. She is brought carefully down a staircase, pushed around a bit. The man's clothes smell like creosote, a door is closed, a lock is bolted, and the man says, "Okay, we're here. You can sit down, take off the bag, whatever."

Sarah takes off the bag. She rubs her chin, indented from the rubber band, but at least she can breathe. She is in a place that is dimly lit. She sees she is in a small room without windows, except for a small opening in the door that faces her. She figures she is in a basement.

The man is behind the door, moving things about. She cannot see his face. She asks, "Please, tell me what is going on?"

The man now has an answer. "You've been kidnapped. If you need a drink of water, there's a sink behind you. Okay, then, settle down."

Sarah is utterly confused. She looks around the room, the cell. A mattress is on the floor. There's a blanket. There's a toilet and sink next to the mattress. It is a bathroom, a bathroom in a basement, with a mattress taking up most of the floor. Sarah feels gratitude she has a toilet at her disposal.

In 2014, before their return to Montpelier, Sarah and Ricky reunited after a trial separation.

Their families had known each other for a long time as Montpelier neighbors. Ricky's older sister Meg and Sarah had gone through school together and Ricky, as a teenager, had surprisingly become friends with Sarah's father, the lawyer Sam Jacobson. The friendship had evolved into a lawyer-client relationship when Ricky needed a lawyer to represent him after he was expelled from high school during his senior year. He was expelled for sending an online message to a lesbian classmate. He'd told her that she was sinning against God. With Sam's professional help, he sued the Montpelier School District for violating his First Amendment right to speak freely about matters of morality and religion.

At the time, Sarah, who had already graduated from Brown University and was living in Providence, Rhode Island, knew Ricky primarily as Meg's kid brother, but she had heard about Ricky's homophobic behavior and she despised him for it. She was also incensed at her father for taking on a case defending ignorant bigotry. She was often aggravated by her father.

Things had changed. Ricky experienced a crisis of guilt over the way he had treated his classmate, his friend, whose body had later been found at the bottom of a cliff. As a result, he left the fundamentalist church to which he'd been devoted.

Later, he and Sarah had met in New York City on the occasion of Sam's argument at the Second Circuit Court of Appeals, a case relating to whether a Vermont town was constitutionally permitted to begin its town meeting every year with a Christian prayer.

Both Sarah and Ricky attended the argument in the downtown Manhattan court, and after the argument they had begun a non-argumentative conversation, first on a bench in Columbus Park near the courthouse, amid pigeons and tai-chi dancers, then continuing over a meal and wine at the noisy sidewalk table of an Italian restaurant on Mulberry Street. The conversation continued over the course of alternating visits in Providence and New York, where Ricky was by then enrolled as an undergraduate at NYU.

What had begun as contempt had changed—bloomed—into something quite the opposite. She was seven years older than he, which had made for an unusual coupling.

Through his college years, they remained in the flush of new love, visiting back and forth between lower Manhattan and the Olneyville neighborhood in Providence. They had an intellectual bond, pushing each other with their ideas, sometimes reading the same books, the same authors. Over one six-month period, they read all the novels of Russell Banks and Richard Russo.

They shared politics too, Ricky having radically adjusted his political sensibilities as he entered college. Together they attended rallies celebrating reproductive freedom, mourning climate change. They watched Rachel Maddow on TV and Amy Goodman online, and phoned each other afterward.

Of course, they didn't agree about all matters. Sarah accused Ricky of being enamored of Obama, while Sarah, closer to the ground and always the more cynical of the two, condemned the administration over its deportation practices.

Beyond all this, their physical bond, their sexual attraction, was magnetically strong; they could not get enough of each other's skin and breath.

In that time, when they saw each other they walked a lot, meandering along the streets of Greenwich Village and Chinatown, or the gritty neighborhoods of Providence. Ricky was a good head taller than Sarah. He modified his usual loping stride to match hers. She looked up at him as they walked, admiring his lean face with deeply set inquisitive eyes, and he would turn to her and wobble to a stop as he looked into her face—a beautiful angelic face, he always told her, her eyes shining, her dimples inviting, the lines around her mouth suggesting mischief.

In both cities, they found hole-in-the-wall eateries that satisfied their culinary passions without emptying their wallets. They favored a Soho establishment called The Hippie Chickpea, specializing in lamb gyros and other Greek or middle eastern fare. Others were Indian or Thai or Senegalese or Guatemalan. Ricky started to cook too.

On a Saturday morning he'd leave Sarah still in bed and make coffee and go out to the fruit and vegetable markets with a backpack. On his return to her Providence apartment, he'd find her still in pajamas, drinking coffee, and he'd take over Sarah's tiny kitchen to make vegetarian meals with brown rice and black beans, tofu sautéed with tamari and nutritional yeast, with chopped peanuts and Swiss chard or snap peas or Brussels sprouts or whatever other fresh vegetable he had found in the markets.

From the kitchen on such a day, they returned to the futon in the bedroom, the sunlight streaming through a dirty window. Sarah lay back with her legs up and let him pull her pajama bottoms off, and she yearned to have this young beautiful man completely inside her, watching him as he pulled off his jeans too, and his shirt and undershirt. She knew him so well, better than she had known any of her other boyfriends, even Tyrene, she was sure of that.

But she was not sure that Ricky knew her quite well enough, or himself; that was the faint shadow over her soul as they made love that day.

As his graduation from NYU approached, they had faced a decision point. Ricky was unsure what to do with his life, how to begin living as an adult. Sarah found herself becoming irritated at Ricky's lack of confidence and initiative. He told her he would like to come live with her, but she was afraid that would be the wrong move. It was too soon, she felt. At least too soon for her.

Or maybe he was too much for her, or too good for her. In fact, she didn't really know the reason, just knew she was irritated, with him and with herself.

Ricky had never had another romantic or sexual relationship. They joked that he had been chaste before Sarah and then chased by Sarah. On the other end of the spectrum, Sarah had had at least a dozen relationships with sex in the mix. One kind of sex or another. The sex usually arose from a casual friendship, most often with men.

Love—what Sarah characterized as love—was an ingredient in only a small handful of her relationships. Ricky was different. Still, the kind of commitment he appeared to want scared her.

"Ricky, I think, I really think," she told him, "we have to try being separate for a while. It's healthy." Sarah did not always recognize how much pain she could cause.

"Why is it healthy? I mean, we are doing well. I am in love with you. You've always told me you love me."

"I do love you, Ricky. But listen, you don't know enough to choose me for good. I've got all sorts of defects and warts. Don't you think you should explore a little?"

They were sitting in a booth in the back of a Providence restaurant, an Italian pizza and pasta place. They could hear the chatter from the kitchen.

"Is that what you want for yourself, Sarah? You want a break? You want to try another relationship?"

"It's not like I have someone in particular in mind," she said.

"So, what then?" he persisted.

"You," she said. "You have to try being in the world without me. Then you'll know more, and we'll see." Their legs bumped under the table.

"Shit, Sarah." And his eyes got teary, and she put her hand over his, and they sat there. She scooted off the bench seat and came around the table to sit next to Ricky, putting her arm around his shoulders. She kissed his neck. A waiter watched them and apparently decided to wait longer before clearing their plates and asking about dessert.

"Who do you love then?" he asked her.

"Ricky!"

"No, Sarah, really, who do you love?"

"I love you," she said. "And maybe others."

"Others," he said.

"I said maybe," she said.

"You used to talk about that guy Tyrene you knew at Brown. Is he one of the maybe-others?"

"Ah, Tyrene," she said. She watched Ricky closely. "Do you want dessert or coffee or anything?"

"No. Well, yeah, I'll have coffee." He signaled to the waiter.

"Maybe Tyrene is one of the maybe-others," she said.

The waiter arrived. "I changed my mind," said Ricky. "Sorry. Sarah, do you want anything?" She shook her head. "We'll take the check," he told the waiter.

"It doesn't sit well with me," he told Sarah. "I feel like you're being selfish."

In the end, after more painful discussions, he did move to Providence, but he found his own apartment and a job as a line cook in the very same restaurant whose booth they had occupied. They still talked often. He told Sarah he was thinking about graduate school and perhaps law school. He bided his time.

He did find another relationship, he confessed to Sarah, with the niece of the restaurant owner. He even told Sarah how the restaurant owner's niece (that's the way they referred to her, not by name) loved to screw on top of the tables after closing. It did not take him long to learn she was using cocaine, a mysterious habit he could not fathom or condone.

He missed Sarah's fresh open face and her moral intelligence. He waited.

For her part, Sarah tried to set Ricky's face and body and mind aside. At the restaurant, Ricky had asked her about Tyrene, her former boyfriend from her student days at Brown University. Tyrene could hardly be more different from Ricky. She decided she wanted to see him. It occurred to her analytic mind that the personality contrast might give her a useful perspective on the level of her own commitment to Ricky. She had no idea if Tyrene would be interested.

She had seen him first in a university classroom during her sophomore year, in early 2006. The subject was Latin America and U.S. intervention. He was a frequent talker in class, expressing his views with precision and anger, and he drew Sarah's admiration. He was tall, like Ricky, but broader in the chest and shoulders, and he perched on the edge of his seat when he spoke in class, as if ready to pounce. He was second-generation American on his father's side; the grandparents had come from Haiti.

He evidently had noticed Sarah too, also an engaged participant in class discussion. "Come and have coffee with me," he told her after class on a winter day.

Sarah threw him a mischievous smile. "You're asking me or telling me?"

"Grammatically, I was telling you," Tyrene responded. "But it is a question. It is my way of asking a question of you."

At the coffeeshop on the edge of campus, he told her, "I like the way you challenge the professor. You make me think deeper."

Sarah flushed. This guy was a senior and he was way better informed than she about the material, and she thought he was smarter too. She learned that colonial history and U.S. imperialism were academic side passions for Tyrene. His major was mathematics, particularly the study of logic and what he called foundations. He had written a paper on Gödel's Incompleteness Theorems, he told her, that had been accepted for publication in the *Journal of Philosophical Logic*.

"That sounds like a big deal," Sarah said.

"No," Tyrene replied, "it's bullshit. It doesn't change anything."

"Then why?"

"Because I love it and I get it and I see stuff others don't. But none of it matters. What matters is changing the material conditions of the world." He frowned at her.

They had a few more after-class coffeeshop rendezvous. Heat between them was building. Sarah was intoxicated by his voice, a soft Texas accent that she imagined retained a lilt of his Haitian French ancestry. She watched his wide lips making his sentences, hard sentences delivered from soft lips in a soft accent. She wanted to progress from coffee and asked him if they could go out for a drink.

"This is a drink," he said, pointing to his mug.

"Sure, Tyrene, but I mean, like, how about a glass of wine together, or a beer?"

"No, I don't drink," he told her.

Sarah pressed him on that, to find out more. He was reluctant to talk, then said, "It makes my depression worse." She probed. He explained he had bipolar disorder, now well under control. "So I won't drink with you," he said. "But I would like to sleep with you." Just like that.

She smiled and blushed. "Wow. That's interesting." She reached across the small table and put her hand on his cheek, then pulled his face toward her. She found his lips and opened them with hers. She pulled away to take a breath. "Oh my," she said.

"You know, I said I'd like to sleep with you, not kiss you in public." But no one around them seemed to be paying attention.

They made love that afternoon in Tyrene's apartment. Sarah was nervous. Even as she discovered he had a softer side beneath the carapace he wore in class, and she was moved by his words and his fingers, she felt she didn't understand him enough. Three more trysts over three successive days, and she was less nervous.

"My Blackness," he observed in his soft voice about this time, "does not seem to be a barrier for you." They had left the Latin America class together and were walking back to his apartment. That is where they went; Sarah shared a house with a group of undergraduates that did not afford a lot of privacy.

There was slush on the street after a rare snowfall. "That surprises you?" she asked. "Of course it's not a barrier."

"No cause for defensiveness, Ms. Jacobson. There is no *of course* about it."

What was she to say? How does one talk about this? She could not tell him his Blackness was irrelevant to her, since it was essential to his being. She thought, too, that maybe his Blackness, far from being irrelevant, was part of the attraction for her. Perhaps she chose him because he was Black, because, with Tyrene on her arm and in her bed, she was ultra-cool, more radical than thou. She was afraid to explore that dark avenue.

Tyrene had called her *Ms. Jacobson* just now, she realized. Perhaps he was making some point about her Jewish identity. She wondered if her Jewishness was essential to *her* being. She concluded it was probably not, although she was sure it was to her parents. And to her grandparents, maternal and paternal, Jacobson and Lowbeer, their Jewishness was everything—at least that was so in 1938 when their families fled Europe.

She cast off that layer and stayed with skin color. "Is my whiteness, or whiteishness, a barrier to you?" she asked him, stepping off a curb to cross the street. She landed in four inches of slush and soaked her foot. She was wearing sneakers. She swore.

"Your taupeishness?" He smiled. She didn't recognize his face when he smiled, it was so rare. It did not convey joy, just ease. "No, it is not," he said. "I can handle that."

What's there to handle? she wondered silently.

He read her expression. "You don't think it's significant," he said. "It is huge, me dating a white lady."

At least I'm a lady. She looked hard at him.

They were regular companions through the winter and spring, while keeping their separate places and spheres, deepening their connection. Tyrene graduated that spring and was admitted into the Brown doctoral program to continue his studies in logic and foundations. That resolved the need for them to decide whether and how to try to make a long-distance relationship work. He was staying in Providence and their shared four months suddenly appeared to have morphed into a Serious Relationship.

When Sarah's parents visited Providence in May, staying at a Holiday Inn, she asked him, "Do you want to meet my parents?"

He asked her what she thought.

"I want you to meet them. Please?"

Tyrene nodded solemnly.

On the phone with her mom, Sarah said, "Good, let's meet for dinner. The Japanese place on Wickenden near Brook Street where we've been before, okay? I'll make reservations. Seven o'clock, okay?" That settled, she said, "I'll bring my friend; his name's Tyrene Jean-Pierre."

Donna repeated the name to be sure she had it right. Sarah could hear her father, listening in, saying the name again, with a question mark, as if verifying if it could be real. "That's his *name*, Sam," her mother whispered.

Tyrene was listening to Sarah's end of the conversation. She was relieved he couldn't hear her parents.

"His grandparents come from Haiti," she explained to her mother. "But he's from Texas; he's a grad student."

Dinner was polite and calm, with careful inquiry about current events and studies and campus life and life back in Montpelier. After their first-course plates were cleared, Sarah placed her hand over Tyrene's hand on the table, for a moment, a signal to her parents about the nature of the relationship. Donna smiled at her warmly; her father wore a perplexed look.

The mishap occurred when it was time for the check. "Let me get this," Sam said. He almost always paid, nothing unusual there. But he added, with a low chuckle, "I don't imagine you have much in the way of resources, Tyrene." It fell flat and awkward, pregnant with presumptions, and sat there in the middle of the table among the used napkins. Sam cleared his throat and signaled for the server.

In a conversation in a coffeeshop the next day, Sam told his daughter that Tyrene Jean-Pierre seemed like a good fellow and he hoped she was happy.

"Yes, I am happy," she said without delving into complications. "Tyrene's so smart. Don't worry about him being Black, Dad."

He scoffed at the thought. "Ach," he muttered, "what's there to worry? This is nothing." Sarah guessed he was falling into Yiddishisms, quite foreign to his usual mode of speech, to demonstrate his understanding of what it means to be a minority, a member of an oppressed class. "The only thing, Sarah, is to ask if he is a good man and a constant man."

Sarah thought about that and was not sure if she could answer the question. She spread cream cheese onto her bagel and sipped her coffee.

Her father noticed her silence. He busied himself with his bagel too and looked at her carefully. He said, "You know, I'm sorry about that thing I said last night about Tyrene's resources when I was paying the bill. I don't know what I was thinking. It was incredibly stupid."

"Okay, Dad," she said. "It's not so bad." What were Tyrene's resources anyway? She didn't know. His apartment was nice enough. A lot of stuff she didn't know.

"You forgive me?" he asked.

Sarah smiled and nodded.

Tyrene, for his part, told her he liked both her parents. "Yeah, they're great, Sarah. Solid politics, solid values. It helps me understand why you are who you are and why I feel about you the way I feel about you. Which is feelings of love."

Feelings of love felt somehow weak to her. Sarah was not sure she wanted to probe deeper on that point. Tyrene quickly added, "I can't be the first person who has told you that you are so much like your father."

"How so?"

"Oh, man, the turns of phrase, the way your eyes sparkle when you say something clever, the mannerisms, the sarcasms." His silky voice was intoxicating her again. She imagined she had heard him say *orgasms* instead of *sarcasms*. She laughed out loud at the absurdity. "Okay, what is that for?" he asked, but she did not tell.

What she said instead was, "I wish I could meet your parents."

He had told her before that would not happen. His parents were divorced. His mother had remarried and started another family with a man Tyrene hated. They lived in Houston. Tyrene had been relieved to flee Houston to start college in New England. Tyrene's father had gone back to Haiti, found his relatives, and stayed.

Sarah was bewildered when, over the following months, Tyrene's personality transformed. He fell into a depression. The phase was deep and closed, and Sarah could not find a way in even to offer comfort. He rebounded, but he became a different person, self-critical, rambling, agitated.

Eight years later, in 2014, a grown-up Sarah had settled into her post-Ricky days. She tried to recollect that painful period with Tyrene in her innocent life. She sat upright on the futon one evening with her laptop and found a folder of Tyrene's emails. She landed on one written in August 2006, the year they had met. She recalled the circumstances. They had spent the previous night together, sometimes clasped tightly in dripping-wet sex and falling off each other, lying back, gasping, sometimes talking, and sleeping too. She recalled they talked a lot that night.

She didn't recall the subjects they talked about. But she recalled, vaguely, a mood of misunderstanding each other, as he shifted into a wound-up gear. She read the email he had sent her the following day:

> I've gotta apologize for my aggression. It's a flaw that has been off-putting in the past, and I have heard, on more than a few occasions, that my aggressive nature of "intensity" has offended or hurt or been counterproductive. Thing is, I got no awareness that I cross the line from, I don't know, "animated" or "energetically engaged" or at worst "exacting" to "demanding" or "aggressive." Despite the impression that my pushiness may have made, PLEASE

> trust that you are my dear, kind, cherished friend, and I have no doubt that you have nothing but good intentions in communicating meaningfully with me. So please know that I (as I write, I realize how condescending my approach is) erroneously and arrogantly think that my relentlessness is benign. I mistakenly believe it is a productive effort to overcome an impasse in understanding by questioning, to hone in on clarity. But I see that it really is my selfish belief that I can advance the discussion by "guiding" another person's ability to more clearly articulate what they mean. Although I really feel like it's a benign effort, it is—I see now—patronizing and presumptuous. That is a bad life practice and only part of my problem.

Sarah began to cry as she read Tyrene's email on her laptop; she saw now how he was losing control of his mind in a way she hadn't seen clearly at the time. That was their impasse in understanding. It wasn't his race, his black skin, his Haitian ancestry; it wasn't his superior intelligence, his mathematical genius, or his political commitments—all things she had wondered about during that period of time, if not that night. No, it was the illness itself, his mania.

She wiped her eyes with her sleeve. His email went on, and on:

> Truly, in the midst of it, I honestly feel there is a "back and forth," that equilibrium exists, and I am simply trying to get at a better articulation of a person's actual thinking when I believe (what an ass I am—this apology is surprisingly revelatory for me) my questions are helping the other person better identify and then better express what they are trying to say. What arrogance! There is a reference in philosophy—as you know (and I'm not trying to be pretentious, but now that I know

> I can talk philosophy with you, although a bit grandi-
> ose, it at least helps me in my mind to be able to refer-
> ence better expressions of my thinking, helpful for ME
> to express myself)—in Buber's "I and Thou" that over-
> states, maybe—my fuck up—but is helpful to me, the
> discussion is helpful, hopefully in convincing you that I
> am seeing what I did and do.

She looked away from the screen.

The email continued. She closed it without reading more.

For a few minutes, she sat on the futon and wondered what to do with herself. On impulse, she clicked open his next email in chronological order. It picked up the same theme:

> Call me on it, Sarah—fucking interrupt me—because I
> really don't know I'm going that far when it happens. I
> do not relieve myself of the responsibility of catching
> myself by asking you, but until I reform, I need help.
> PS, also, I don't mean to be bombastic. I am driven by
> the process involved in the effort to best express the
> wonder of ideas, feelings, emotions—vital to existing
> as a thoughtful being by making and diligently seek-
> ing clarity (perhaps in my case arcane to the point of
> annoyance), but you can see that the art of commu-
> nicating the esoteric, subjective aspects of life evades
> me. I so love you, my cherished friend.

Sarah stopped on his ending phrase, *I so love you, my cher-
ished friend*, absorbing his expression of love for her. She got up and did a small pirouette and went to the kitchen to pour herself a glass of chardonnay. She meandered back to the futon.

She pulled an afghan over herself and imagined Tyrene's face. She suppressed his illness, his destructiveness. She remembered the shape of his body, the smell of his skin, the hardness of his mascu-linity. She masturbated and fell asleep.

Awakening a short time later, Sarah was momentarily confused. Her open laptop beside her on the futon brought back what she had been doing, and her mouth tasted bitter. She got up, went to the bathroom, wandered aimlessly for a minute or two. She needed to make sense of her memories.

Maybe she had saved texts from Tyrene during that time? She picked up her cellphone from the table by the apartment's entry door. She found a text message from late September of 2006, the beginning of her junior year at Brown:

> Maybe you cannot relate to my disregard for certain forms of decorum, in modesty, language, loud resistance, purposely uncensored references to the raw, savage, or even sublimely erotic aspect of life.

Yes, she could relate, and she had wanted some of it for herself. Some of it, but not too much of it. Another text from a month later in the oscillations of Tyrene's bipolar life:

> I wrote all that because I'm compulsively expressive and landed in the wrong place in life. We need not discuss anything but, rather, I will invent some way to make you laugh.

Sarah did smile at this, sitting on her futon in the front room, eight years later. *Landed in the wrong place in life.* She pictured Tyrene saying it, could hear his voice saying it. In what place in life had he landed now?

Sarah had pulled away from him. At the time, her reasons were not so apparent to her. She was ignorant about his bipolarism. She knew she was frustrated that he wouldn't give her a straight answer when she asked him if he had stopped taking his meds. She knew she'd been fearful.

Tyrene did not blame her. He offered her an out. She found the text where he wrote:

> If this friendship, like every single relationship in my
> life, ends up being a lie, it will harm me. So, I will make
> it easy—just text me and say four words: I am not com-
> ing.

She did not send such a text, and it did not end there. Sarah
tried a little longer, but then he wrote:

> My entire life is a waste of time and a lie. I AM CRAZY.
> FUCKING NUTS. JUST STAY AWAY.

No longer an offer, it was an edict. When a lover commands
you to stay away, do you obey, or do you persevere? Which path
do you choose?

Eventually she had succumbed to describing Tyrene's condition
to her parents. Donna asked her questions about his symptoms and
asked how the relationship made Sarah feel. But she would not tell
Sarah what to do. "Follow your heart. You'll know what's right."

Her father, on the other hand, was liberal with his advice. "He's
right, Sarahkins, you should back off. Not as a friend. You can be
his friend if you can handle the emotions. And if he lets you. But
don't try to make a life with him. Don't try to have a relationship.
You'd regret it terribly."

"We *have* a relationship."

"Well, I mean, don't try to take it further. You don't need that
in your life."

"All right, enough, Dad."

"Huh? Oh, I see, you don't need my advice."

"No, it's okay, but I've heard it before. And, right, I'm not
really looking for your advice. I just wanted to talk about it." Her
father often seemed to take up too much space.

The path she chose in the fall of her junior year at Brown was
to stay away from Tyrene. They lost touch. She didn't know what
had happened to him, except she later learned he had dropped out
of the PhD program.

Sarah was young and healthy and a college student; she was miserable for only a month. Coursework demanded her time. A guy named Harris marched happily into her life. She and Harris became active in the Occupy movement on the streets of Providence. So occupied herself, Sarah left Tyrene behind.

But over the months and then in the years that followed, the feeling that she had been a strange combination of shallow and hard-shelled periodically intruded into her conscious mind.

After Ricky and she separated, the time had come to check in again with Tyrene, perhaps to apologize, or to accept an apology. Perhaps to find their way back into each other. Sarah found his number and tried it. Tyrene answered.

He seemed curious to hear from her out of the blue after so many years, and he agreed to meet. Sarah was pleased and very nervous. She suggested a breakfast rendezvous at a trendy bistro that served exotic juices and fare such as omelets with chèvre and morels.

Sarah got there on time. Tyrene texted to say he'd be twenty minutes late. Sarah made the mistake of a second espresso while she waited, and it made her jumpy. She saw him come in through the door. He had grown dreadlocks that spiked high above his head.

When he came over to her table, he had trouble looking her in the eye. She realized she had chosen an utterly wrong venue. They should have met in a quiet unpretentious place.

He was manic, yes, but also appeared to be paranoid, something she hadn't seen clearly before. He was flying with ideas about the racist world conspiring to defeat him. He was angry and his posture implied that he placed her, his former lover, in an enemy camp of conspirators. He told her that everyone wanted to harm him and every other Black man too. There were threats everywhere.

This wasn't something she could argue with, as a white woman sitting across from a Black man whose life experience would always be distant from hers. At a loss, she asked stupidly, "Real threats?"

"You shitting me? Of course, they're real. Pay attention, Sarah! I walk down the road. Every white guy I meet wants to fuck with me. I got no freedom to live." He spoke with a metallic edge. The soft voice she had fallen for was gone.

A couple of gay men at the next table were arguing about the distinction between beer and ale. Tyrene turned on them. "Fucking idiots, what fucking difference does it make. Don't you see what's going on around you?"

They looked shattered and had no response.

Sarah paid the bill and ushered Tyrene out of the restaurant. They parted on the sidewalk. They did not hug, and Sarah retreated with a bruised heart.

Three months after their separation had begun, Ricky came knocking at her door. Sarah opened it and let him back in.

Ricky had never treated her or anyone else with meanness. Ricky was not mentally ill. He was sane and calm, a quiet deep ocean. It was not as if Ricky had escaped all complications. He had not. His growth away from the fundamentalist church and its teachings showed that much. But he had landed, she believed, more or less in the right place in life.

"You feel so familiar," he told her.

"And you," she said. "We are so fucking different. Are you sure you want to try this?"

"Language!" he scolded, sounding like his mother.

"That's just what I mean," she said, "so fucking different."

"Difference is good, right?"

Difference was good.

They made a life, a portion of a life. Sharing the small apartment. Living inexpensively. Sarah an organizer, Ricky at the restaurant. For the moment.

Then came the news just a few months after Ricky's return, shattering Sarah's peace of mind. Tyrene had been killed. By coincidence, her father was the one who learned about it and the one to phone Sarah.

As he later explained to his daughter, Sam had attended an event at Yale Law School in January of 2015. He was a graduate of the school and maintained friendships with faculty members. He also liked, Sarah knew, to hobnob with eminent legal scholars. Sam attended his class reunions periodically and also the occasional seminar, and once had been invited as a speaker at a seminar on religion and civil society.

The 2015 event was a colloquium on campaign finance reform and the First Amendment. During a break between sessions, he had wandered into the law school's dining hall and there picked up a copy of the New Haven Register someone had left on a table. Thumbing through it, he came across an article describing the killing of Tyrene Jean-Pierre by a New Haven police officer. *Shooting*, the headline declared, *Ruled Justifiable*.

Sam sucked in his breath, clenched his teeth, and glanced around him. A group was at the next table with Professor Akash Dhandi; one of them was talking animatedly about the *Citizens United* case. Sam felt he needed solitude and full concentration to absorb this awful thing in front of him, and he moved to another table.

Mr. Jean-Pierre, originally from Houston, the article reported, had approached and confronted two officers who were in a parked cruiser on Whalley Avenue. He was yelling and belligerent, according to the officers. The officers told him to back off and go on his way. He did not obey. When Tyrene leaned in the open window of the cruiser, one of the officers used a taser on him. But the taser did not sufficiently disable Tyrene, who was then, according to the officers, raving incoherently and brandishing a knife at the officer who had tased him. Three shots were fired into Tyrene's chest by the same officer. Tyrene died instantly.

A witness on the nearby sidewalk told investigators she did not see a knife. Her testimony was deemed unreliable, perhaps because the witness had an addiction disorder. There was no video or audio recording of the incident.

Mr. Jean-Pierre was in New Haven, the article reported, to seek treatment for his psychiatric condition. The diligent reporter had tracked down a former colleague of the shooting victim in the Brown University Mathematics Department in Providence, Rhode Island, who, himself suffering from a psychiatric disorder, had helped get a referral for Tyrene. He was planning to see a specialist at Yale-New Haven Hospital. Tyrene was feeling very hopeful about the prospects of the new treatment, according to the Brown professor.

Sam Jacobson put the newspaper down and made a call to his daughter.

The man who is holding Sarah in the little room in the basement thinks his idea is strong and smart. His brain is one of his muscles and he has exercised it. He will hold his Jewish princess until the lawsuit is over.

At first, he thought they couldn't prove their case without her there, and the case would be thrown out of court just for that reason. That's what Marty Frazier, the dumb fuck from True Patriots, told him.

But that's just it: Marty's a dumb fuck.

The man's brother tells him Marty is wrong about this because they have other witnesses. There's the Jewish lawyer and the kid,

Manny. His brother says you have to do more. You have to let them know you're holding her and you'll hurt her if they don't dismiss the case. His brother says they have to dismiss the case *with prejudice*.

"What does that mean?" he asks his brother.

His brother tells him that means they dismiss it for good, and he knows about the law. So the man decides that is what he'll do.

On a cool day in October 2017, almost three years after Tyrene's death, Sarah was sitting on a bench in the scrappy park next to her workplace on Manton Avenue, in Providence. She wore blue jeans and a red jacket filled with some kind of microfiber, zipped up over a scarf. She faced the busy road with her cellphone in her hand and an egg salad sandwich on a sheet of wax paper in her lap.

Traffic whizzed by, and the sun that cleared the buildings on the southern side of the street warmed her body. She scrolled through her emails, reading some, saving a few, discarding most. In the Human Rights Network newsletter, she noticed a posting for a job at an organization called Green Mountain Black Lives Matter.

Looking to her right down the street, she saw a family with a stroller on the sidewalk at the end of the block, heading slowly in her direction. She watched them briefly and returned her attention to the phone. She followed a link in the job posting to a website for Green Mountain BLM. It was a newly formed Vermont organization that was looking to hire a staff person to be its "youth organizing coordinator."

Sarah knew there were other BLM organizations active in Vermont. This one appeared to be focused on middle and high school students. There was movement in the hills of Vermont.

The family on the sidewalk came closer to her. They were Hispanic-looking, probably Guatemalan, she thought, like many of her clients. The mother was pregnant. At this moment, the man crouched down to fix a wheel on the stroller that had gone kinky.

Sarah smiled and waved to the toddler in the stroller, but she didn't think the girl saw her.

On the sidewalk to her left, Sarah noticed three young men with barrel chests. They had a kind of rolling, side-to-side gait that made her think they were proud of their masculinity.

Sarah worked for a neighborhood non-profit, coordinating campaigns to organize local residents in the Latinx community on issues relating to immigration, workplace abuses, and foreclosures. But internal divisions embroiled the organization. Meetings had become awful yelling experiences. Some who professed a passion for equity and inclusion engaged in the worst personal attacks.

Sarah didn't see much light through the tunnel her workplace had become. On top of that, she hadn't been paid for three months, as expected funds had not materialized from granting agencies and donors. She was ready to jump. The whole thing made her sad.

The wind picked up. Putting her phone down beside her, careful to balance the sandwich on her lap, she pulled the scarf up around the back of her head. Her scarf was Guatemalan, given to her by a member of her organization.

Sarah had grown up in Montpelier, Vermont's small capital city, and she wondered about returning home and whether Ricky would want to make the move. Sarah was the only daughter of Donna and Sam Jacobson, parents whom she loved and fought with and had needed space away from. Ricky had grown up in Montpelier too. Ricky's parents, Clara and Carver Stillwell, were conservative Baptists, a rarity in Montpelier. That was complicated for Ricky. Now there's an understatement, she thought, smiling.

One of the young men on the sidewalk to her left wore a T-shirt that said *White Motherfucker*, words that she could read as they approached, but embroiled in her own thoughts, she couldn't understand their meaning at first. All three men wore baseball-type hats. They were red, and Sarah now saw they were emblazoned with the MAGA letters, *Make America Great Again*.

The kneeling Guatemalan man, if that is what he was, stood up from his stroller repair, looking at the three white men who were still walking toward the family, about thirty or forty feet away. Sarah could see him then glance down at the girl in the stroller, who was probably his daughter. The street was busy with traffic. The father looked for a break in the traffic.

Sarah squinted into the sun's glare and watched the little family, her egg salad sandwich still on her lap as she clutched her phone. If not for the sandwich on her lap, she would later think, she might have gotten up, to do something. She didn't know what it was she might have done.

An opening appeared in the traffic and the family stepped onto the road. The stroller wheel was still not functioning well and veered to the side, so the father picked up the little girl with his right arm and lifted the stroller off the pavement in his left hand. The woman held onto his arm, and they tried to cross. It all took too long.

By the time they reached the middle of the road, cars were coming fast in the opposite lane. Five cars sped close by them as they huddled in the middle of the street, horns blaring on all sides. Over the traffic noise, Sarah could hear the toddler, who had begun crying.

Sarah felt rooted to the bench, watching, gasping, as a moment later a gap in the traffic appeared in the far lane and the family rushed across to the other side, the father dragging the stroller behind him as he held the girl and the mother's arm.

Before they made it clear to the far sidewalk, a delivery truck with its horn pealing slammed the stroller, which flew from the man's hand. The truck didn't stop. The stroller, airborne, clattered to the gutter on the road's edge. One of the wheels was knocked free and kept rolling down the street.

The MAGA-hat guys had reached the pavement in front of Sarah, and she could hear their deep male chuckling. Across the street, the family on the far sidewalk, apparently uninjured, reassembled themselves.

Both parties continued on their separate ways as Sarah sat still on the bench and watched. The traffic on Manton hummed.

Sarah let her breath slow down. She ate her egg salad sandwich, carefully, so nothing would fall into her lap. She turned back to her phone and finished reading about Green Mountain Black Lives Matter and the new job. She decided she would talk with Ricky that evening.

She and Ricky had take-out Thai and beer in the room they called the front room because it overlooked the street. Their tiny apartment was on the second floor. Nine people currently occupied the four apartments in the rambling Victorian building.

They sat on an upright futon, the half-filled cartons of noodles and Massaman curry on the low table in front of them. "That would be a huge change, Sarah." They sipped from the bottles. "I do miss Montpelier." Ricky finished his beer, holding his head back for the last of it, his Adam's apple bobbing. He set down the bottle and looked at her. "Let's do it."

Sarah gazed at him. "Just like that? Shouldn't we see if I get the job first?"

"Yes, we should see about that." He was a bit tipsy.

"Do you think they'd hire a white person?" she asked him.

"Why not?"

"Don't be a doofus, Ricky. Race matters for a job like this."

"Okay," he acknowledged.

"What about you, Ricky? About the move?"

"I really miss living in Vermont," he told her. "I miss the fields. I miss the space and the woods. You know, I want to have a garden. I want a backyard. And maybe I'd like to be closer to my parents."

"That surprises me a bit. Really?"

"Yuh, really. Time goes on. For me right now, Providence feels too tight. Too many of us walking on top of each other. Do you ever feel that way, Sarah?"

"No, I don't think so. Maybe I'm more of an urban person than you." She smiled at Ricky. She watched him studying her; he looked at her mouth, the dimples around her mouth.

He raised his gaze to her eyes again. "Maybe we want to start a family some time?"

"Oh?"

They stared at each other.

"Do you think we'd get married first?" Sarah asked.

"I hadn't thought about marriage," he answered. "I do think about a family. Do you?"

She looked at him, perplexed. "Work?" she asked.

He accepted the pivot. "I still don't know about that, Sarah. I won't miss my job here. I'll figure it out. I'll find something. Don't rightly know about the long term."

"Don't *rightly* know? You sound like an English schoolboy."

He just grinned at her.

"Come over here, schoolboy," she said. They kissed. They brought the cartons and bottles to the kitchen and put the leftovers in the fridge. Ricky rinsed the bottles and tossed them in the recycle bucket. They smiled at each other some more.

They walked to the bedroom, her hand caressing his bottom as he preceded her along the short hallway made especially narrow by bookcases on both sides. In the bedroom, she put one arm around him and caressed his crotch where his cock now perked up and bobbed like his Adam's apple.

She stopped. "You said something just now, that people here are crowding too close to one another."

"I guess I feel that way, Sarah. You don't, I know."

"Something happened on the street today that I want to tell you about."

"Oh?"

"Yes. I'm sorry. Would you like another beer?"

"Another beer? No."

"Okay. I'm going to make tea though. Do you want some tea?"

"Um, no thanks."

"I need to take my time."

"All right," he said. "There's no hurry. There rarely is."

They walked back to the kitchen and Sarah lit the burner and put the kettle on. Ricky sat at the table and watched her. "What is it you want to tell me?"

"It's just that I was eating my lunch in that little park on Manton and I saw something I didn't like at all."

"Yeah?"

"This family of Guatemalans, I think, was there on the sidewalk, a couple and a little girl in a stroller, and the mother was pregnant. They were walking on the sidewalk, kind of approaching where I was sitting from the right. Picture that, okay?"

"Where were you?"

"On a bench in the park, but facing Manton, close to the road. Then three big white guys with MAGA hats showed up on the sidewalk on the left."

The kettle whistled. Sarah put some loose green tea in a strainer and poured through it.

"And what happened?" asked Ricky.

Sarah told him how the family crazily crossed the street, and the stroller got clipped by the truck. "They were terrified, Ricky. I could see this on their faces. The mother was crying. They had to flee across a busy street."

"Awful," said Ricky.

"It's becoming clearer to me, Ricky. This is not their city, not their country. The big white guys owned the street and they laughed as they walked on by. They laughed, Ricky."

"Maybe nothing would have happened if they'd just kept walking along the sidewalk, right?"

"Sure, maybe," she said. She held up the mug and smelled the tea and inhaled the steam. "But they chose to cross through traffic rather than face these men. You're sure you don't want some?"

He shook his head about the tea. "I can see why it upset you," he said.

"I was frozen there on my park bench. I didn't get up. I didn't say anything. I was reading stupid emails and eating a sandwich. Fucking Christ, what a country."

The interview was an informal affair on a Saturday, three months later, at the Sacred Grounds Café, a popular coffee roastery, bistro, and meeting venue on Chamber Street in Montpelier. Sarah got there early. She found an empty table on the river side of the building, where she could look out above the frost on the window at the ducks maneuvering back and forth from the flowing waters of the North Branch of the Scape River to the ice and rocks on the other side.

She took off her oversized coat, hat, and mittens, ordered a coffee and brought the steaming mug to the table. It was a good twenty-five degrees colder here than in Providence. The tabletop was a piece of plexiglass covering a layer of roasted coffee beans spread out on a rough burlap fabric. Its earthiness was supposed to be grounding, she surmised, but its resemblance to a transparent beehive made her queasy. Driving up I-93 and I-89 to get to Montpelier, she had felt totally at ease with a Toots and the Maytals CD keeping her company, but now her confidence waned in the face of those coffee beans. She looked out at the ducks again.

Sarah had a half hour to kill. She pulled out her current book, *A Colony in a Nation* by Chris Hayes—based in part on Hayes's reporting from Ferguson, Missouri. She looked around the coffeehouse. There, on the other side, sat the same group of aging guys (with one woman among them) whom she thought she remembered seeing in the same place years earlier. She imagined they were having the same conversation.

She checked herself for being judgmental, an unfortunate trait she was now grown-up enough to recognize. One of her former high school teachers, now retired, entered the café. The teacher recognized Sarah and came over to her table.

"Sarah Jacobson? Am I right? It's been so long. How are you?" said John Carruthers, who apparently remembered Sarah well. He used to teach physics. He wore suspenders over a gut that had grown too large. He used to drink too much, Sarah remembered. He put his newspaper down on her table and they shook hands.

"I'm really good, Mr. Carruthers, how are you?"

"Oh, call me John," he said. "I can't complain, retired for a few years now, finding this and that to do. I come here to find company, you know? Thank goodness, well maybe thank the teachers' union, for a decent pension. What brings you back to town, and remind me where you've been? Or are you always here?"

Sarah told him where she'd been and briefly what she'd done. Brown University, Providence, community organizing. "And I'm about to have an interview now for this new organizing gig here." She explained about Green Mountain BLM.

"Hey," said Carruthers, "I just read an article about that in the *Times Argus*. Here, take a look." He indicated the paper. "It's on the front page. I'll just get my coffee."

"Sure," she said. "Thank you."

John Carruthers walked over to the counter to place an order. Sarah held her mug of coffee close to her face and started to read.

> Montpelier High School may be the first public school in America to fly the Black Lives Matter flag in support of racial harmony in education in the Capital City. The MHS principal said he did an online search and could not find reference to another public school in the country that flies the BLM flag. 'We may be the first,' he said. The decision to allow the BLM flag to be flown follows

a yearlong effort to address issues of 'systemic racism'
in the Montpelier school system, led by the student
organization Racial Justice Alliance.

"Why do they put *systemic racism* in quotes?" she muttered.

"What's that?" asked Carruthers, who'd returned with a steaming mug. "Can I sit? While you wait, you know. Would that be all right?" He squeezed into the chair across from her.

"Of course. Please do. I'm early for the interview. See, here," she pointed to the text. "They put this term in quote marks. As if systemic racism's a fictional thing."

"Hah! Good point, young critic. Or maybe the quotes are just used to show it's a current term of art, you know?" He smiled at her, tried his coffee, still too hot.

"But it's not," argued Sarah. "It's just a descriptive term of reality—systemic racism, institutional racism. Putting it in quotes is a false nod to neutrality. Journalists are supposed to report the truth."

"And tell both sides of a story," countered Carruthers.

"Yes, yes. All sides. But then settle on the truth. Systemic racism is the truth." Sarah's voice sounded heated. "It's not like the evidence supports two equally legitimate conclusions: on the one hand, that systemic racism pervasively exists in this country; and on the other, that it doesn't exist. Follow the evidence and tell the truth."

"Someone once said," mused Carruthers, "that the truth is not found halfway between right and wrong."

"Yes! That's a good way of putting the point. You wouldn't find an article, to make a blunt comparison, giving equal weight to flat-earth theories."

"Oh, you might in some corners."

"But not in serious journalism," Sarah persisted.

"That's the rub," he said. "The word *serious*. Do you think it's question-begging?"

"Slightly," she acknowledged, smiling at this man who once taught her physics.

"Can we agree, Sarah," asked Mr. Carruthers, holding his mug aloft, "not to lose sight of the main thing about this *Times Argus* story? This is the first flag of this kind at any public school in the country. That is a huge accomplishment."

"Yes, I'm sorry, Mr. Carruthers. I get carried away. You are right, of course."

"John," he corrected. "No need to be sorry! It's a fabulous point you made. Keep reading."

Sarah nodded. "It says here that Vermont was the first state to abolish slavery in its constitution, and the first to enroll and graduate a black student who subsequently served in the state legislature. I knew the first fact, but not the second."

"Me neither," said the retired teacher.

"This part is interesting," said Sarah. "The school superintendent is quoted here, and he says other groups could ask the board for permission to fly a flag that expresses their views, but the board would have to decide if it aligned with the school district's values."

"I noticed that," said Carruthers. "Seems like they're trying to find a way not to have to lend the school's flagpole to just anyone who wants to send a message—like a flat-earther! They're worried about the precedent, don't you think?"

They were interrupted when someone asked, "Are you Sarah Jacobson?"

"Oh my god, I'm so sorry," she said, looking up. "Yes, that's me."

John Carruthers stood up. "So nice to talk with you, Sarah. I'll leave you with the paper."

"You too, John. It was a pleasure seeing you." Sarah turned her attention to her visitors.

There were three; a white man and two young women, one Black and the other maybe Latina. "I thought it was you because of that book on your table," the Black woman said, pointing to the

Chris Hayes book. She introduced herself as Samantha Janey. "It gave you away!"

Sarah laughed and immediately felt at ease.

They made brief introductions by name, placed their drink orders at the service counter, and rejoined Sarah at the table.

"Our organization is new," Samantha Janey explained right off. "But the history goes back. A group of students at U-32 started out organizing around racial justice issues in the last few years. They applied for a grant last spring to turn it all up a notch, yeah, and the grant came through in November. I got hired as the coordinator." Samantha smiled.

Sarah knew U-32 was the middle and high school that served the five small towns immediately surrounding Montpelier. She'd learned the organization's history from her readings about the group. She nodded and sipped her coffee, now lukewarm, asking Samantha, "You were a student there at some point? Or?"

"I graduated from U-32 three years ago and went to Marlboro College down near Brattleboro, but I'm taking this year off, you know, and got hired for this." Samantha paused to check the service counter, but there was no sign yet of their orders. "We're psyched."

"Me too," said Sarah.

"Chip Skinner here, he's the faculty advisor at U-32." Samantha gestured to the thin man at the table, who wore a graying blonde ponytail and now nodded and smiled politely. Sarah was attracted to his kind eyes. "He's the one, really, who oversaw the grant. And Elena here, she's a junior right now at U-32 and is really a key player. She's amazing. The three of us are on the nonprofit board. There are two other students, one in Montpelier and one at U-32, and a couple of others. One of the Montpelier city councilors has joined the board."

"I saw that from the website. It's unusual to have staff—like you—on the board."

"Yeah. It's cool with us, but I know not everyone does it that way."

The person at the counter called out a name, and Samantha and Chip got up to get their drinks. Elena told Sarah she wasn't having anything right now. "Actually, I hate coffee," she confided.

"You could get something else."

"I'm good." They smiled and the others returned.

Samantha banged her large latte on the table. "We're hoping U-32 can follow Montpelier with the flag. Yeah? The group there's been active with justice issues for a long time. And now," Samantha took a quick breath, "we're like cross-pollinating among the Vermont schools. There're groups organizing in Brattleboro, Rutland, and Winooski. We're helping them get going. It's already happened in Burlington and South Burlington. You read the material we sent, right?"

Sarah nodded. "Yes, all of it."

Samantha pushed on. "There's so much momentum, like here and now. We need a state-wide organizer for the high schools. And we have the funds to hire for that. We really liked your stuff and the work you're doing in Rhode Island with immigrant communities. It's terrific. Plus, you're from here. We're kind of amazed you want to come back here, though."

"Oh? My partner and I decided it might be best for us, each for our own reasons maybe. For me, this opportunity popped up and felt right."

"Totally," said Samantha.

They wanted to understand more about Sarah's commitment to the BLM movement. She talked about her years as an organizer in Providence and shared her observations on the intersections of race and policing, incarceration, poverty, neglect in schools. She referred to the "pipeline from school to jail" for Black boys selectively disciplined in school, dropping out and facing few good choices. "Speaking of race," she segued, "I guess I should ask you, you know, about the idea of Black or POC leadership in an organization like this and how a white organizer fits that vision?"

"Glad you brought that up." Samantha grinned at Elena and turned back to Sarah. "We talked on that. We could go either way. We get it. For one thing, we're like an equal opportunity employer and can't take race into account." Here she glanced at Mr. Skinner, who cocked an unruly eyebrow and nodded slowly. "But anyway, I feel white folks need to take responsibility in the Black Lives Matter movement and in all racial justice work. You want to add something, Elena?"

"I guess I feel," Elena spoke softly and carefully, "you'll be going into schools where most all the kids are white. Maybe you can bridge some gaps in a way that might be harder for a BIPOC."

"It's not a bad message," Samantha amplified, "for someone who looks like you to introduce the organization, the movement. That's my view. Maybe not everyone feels that way. I think you'll have success in reaching students, I mean white students, where others might not. What Elena said. What do you think?"

"Yuh, that makes enough sense to me. I see my role as an organizer, not the face of the movement. When it comes to communicating with the public, I'll stand behind others. And I'll listen to you and take direction from you." Sarah was looking at Samantha.

"Ha!" said Samantha.

"And from the student organizers," added Sarah. Sarah liked Samantha more and more. "I am so fired up for this work," she told them.

"And this kind of role isn't new for you," Samantha said. "I mean, in Providence, your work was to organize so folks in the Latinx community could have their voices heard. You've been doing this for years."

"Right, that's true, I have." Sarah sat up straight.

"You know what you're doing," said Elena. "I think that's the kind of experience we need."

They talked some more about the organization and the expectations of the job. Sarah then told them this all seemed really good. "Can I ask, have you interviewed others?"

"We did one interview already." Samantha did a quick eye check with Elena and Chip. "That may not pan out. Hey, can you give us just a minute so we can talk—sorry to be awkward."

"No, no, of course," said Sarah, and she got up and wandered to the other side of the café. She admired the artwork hung on the opposite wall, botanical and bird studies in watercolor by a local painter, Susan Bull Riley. John Carruthers was sitting at the table with the group of aging Boomers Sarah had noticed earlier. He leaned toward her and asked what she thought of them. "The people I'm meeting with for the interview? I like them."

"That's good, but I meant the watercolors."

"Oh!" She laughed. "Exquisite!"

"Yes, aren't they? Look at the milkweed pods going to seed in that one. How a person can capture such delicacy on paper, it's beyond me."

Milkweed seeds squeezed out of their pods and floated into neighboring communities, looking for a promising place to germinate. "They bring me a sense of tremendous serenity," Sarah declared. "I will need it."

"Hey Sarah," she heard, and she returned to the window table. Samantha stood up. "When do you think you can start?"

In her basement cell, alone, Sarah lies on the mattress on the floor. The blanket is pulled up around her. She dozes in and out of sleep. She thinks about Ricky most of all. How can he possibly manage this? They are a team, they take care of each other, and now she has abandoned him. No, not abandoned him, her waking mind tells her, but right off she is back into a dream where it is all her fault, she is suing everyone and everyone is mad at her, and Ricky especially, sweetest Ricky, turns away from her.

She thinks, or perhaps dreams, about Tyrene and his manic and depressive world. She mixes up his paranoia with her own state of fear and blame. In an awake moment, she knows Tyrene is dead, but then she is in the dream again where Tyrene is with her and touching her and making love with her to ward off their fears.

Tyrene tells her soothingly that she is only imagining the bad things she feels. They are figments, he tells her. But approaching the edge of wakefulness, she knows Tyrene is wrong. She knows she is a prisoner in a cell. She can hear the man moving outside the door.

The man talks to her through the door.

Awake, Sarah stands up and looks through the opening. The man is wearing a mask now, a Halloween mask of Donald Trump. She has never seen the man's real face, except a momentary sideways glimpse when they were at her car.

In his Trump mask, her captor holds out a Tupperware container. "Here," he says, "I brought you some food. It's a cheese and tomato sandwich." He holds the container halfway through the opening.

Sarah takes it and says, "Thank you."

At the end of January 2018, in a rented U-Haul truck heading north on I-93, Sarah read out loud to Ricky from another article by the same reporter in the online *Times Argus*. "Listen to this, Ricky," she said. "'Montpelier High School has been swept up in a media frenzy including hate speech and threatening messages on social media after announcing it will fly the Black Lives Matter flag at the request of students concerned about "systemic racism" in the school system.'"

She stopped and said, "There it is in quotes again!"

Ricky, driving, glanced at her. "What?"

"Systemic racism. The reporter puts it in quotes."

"So?" said Ricky. "This matters to you?"

"It's like he doesn't quite believe it's a real thing. It drives me fucking crazy."

Ricky looked at her.

"Never mind," she said. "Watch the road!"

They'd packed their belongings and meager furniture into the U-Haul to make their way to Montpelier—specifically, to a newly renovated apartment above the hardware store on Sproul Street.

"Sarah, I'm interested in the part about hate speech and threats. Keep reading?"

"'School officials announced last week it may be the first public school in the country to fly the BLM flag to support students struggling with racism in school. The news attracted wide attention from local and national news outlets, as well as messages of support. But there was also a strong backlash, with an overwhelming wave of calls, emails, and postings on social media prompting school officials to notify law enforcement.'"

"Backlash," mused Ricky. "Serious, you think?"

"I don't know how serious it is," she answered. "Here's what the paper says: 'School officials said efforts to promote racial harmony at Montpelier High School prompted many messages of sympathy and support, but has also unleashed a strong backlash of hate speech, racial animosity and threats in online forums.' It quotes the superintendent to the effect that this reaction only reinforces their determination to combat racism."

"Good for him," Ricky interrupted. "I'm not being sarcastic."

"You're never sarcastic, Ricky. There's a bit more. Should I keep reading?"

"Definitely," he said, as he negotiated some backed-up traffic on the highway.

"The superintendent says—this is good—that this is an effort to recognize that the experience of students of color in Montpelier schools is not the same as the experience of their white counterparts."

"It's progress. I wonder what you're walking into, though," said Ricky.

It snowed for the last half of the drive and kept snowing the whole time they unloaded the truck with the help of two old friends of Ricky's. The misery of that experience was relieved by the four of them sharing a bottle of Jamieson's Irish Whiskey that Sarah's father had presented to them upon their arrival.

At 9:30 a.m. on February 1, Sarah and her new boss, Samantha Janey, joined a crowd in the parking lot outside the Montpelier High School to witness the raising of the Black Lives Matter flag. The morning sky was deep blue. There were hundreds of people, students and parents and others from the community.

The so-called alt-right backlash had been vigorous, with outlandish false claims that the BLM movement advocated violence against police. Concerns over right-wing violence against the BLM activists explained a police cruiser parked at the entrance to the school and a snowplow blocking access to the parking lot.

A girl, a student, spoke. Sarah knew her as one of the organizers. "What I hope from this ceremony is that it starts a precedent for other schools, local and in the U.S., to better their curriculum for Black students." She said people had called her brave for her advocacy. "But I would also like to recognize that it takes a community that is ready to listen to us and takes up the fight."

The student talked about her school and her education. "Black students, as a whole, are pretty much robbed of a thorough education," she said. "We don't get to go to school learning about ourselves. We are fed a whitewashed curriculum that is not fully representative of American history." She paused as the wind blew across the lot.

"Many people have asked why we're raising the flag today," she continued. "The reason goes back to why people have flags in the first place. People choose their flags because they want to be represented and want to be seen, and we students do not feel like we are represented or seen in our education, and we're here to raise the flag and we want to be seen and we will demand to be represented in our education."

Aretha Franklin was then piped through a speaker, singing the Nina Simone and Weldon Irvine song, "To Be Young, Gifted, and Black." Sarah listened, glad the student was being seen now, was being represented now.

The school principal spoke next. He was humble and admitted he had enjoyed the benefits of being white. He pledged to do his best to ensure a welcome and inclusive school environment. "With your help, I'm learning to better understand my own privilege and the important role I play in the responsibility of ensuring safety, opportunities, and justice for those who do not share any or all those privileges," said the principal.

He looked around the crowd. Sarah kept watching from the edge. "Thank you for understanding," he said, "that the decision to fly a Black Lives Matter flag this month at Montpelier High School is not anti-police; it is anti-bias. Thank you for understanding that we reject any purported violence that some seek to associate with Black Lives Matter, and embrace the message of equity for all."

The crowd was silent as the American flag was lowered. The BLM flag was attached and students took turns raising the two flags together.

Another Black student, whom Sarah had not yet met, took the mic and spoke to the broader community. "We want you to look at the Montpelier High School's Black Lives Matter flag as the continuation of action for educational justice for Black students in our community today and going forward into the future. This flag is a statement of support for Black students in every school in this country and a rallying call for real action to be taken against institutional racism and injustice."

And still another student followed. "I hope that no matter who you are," she said, "every time you walk into this school you can glance at the flag and know that the people in this school know your value and care about you, and that you're not alone in the fight for social justice. We hope that, as you move forward through the rest of your day and the rest of your life, you will always remember this moment in your hearts."

Sarah had grown up in Montpelier and gone to this school, not too many years before. What had she done to challenge white supremacy when she was in high school? Nothing. She had been silent.

There had been about twenty Black or POC students at the time, she thought—mostly South or East Asian, she couldn't really remember—and she simply didn't know what those students had felt at the time. A few had been her friends, but she had not talked about race with them, not directly, and they had not tried to raise the subject with her.

No, maybe that's not right; maybe they had, and she hadn't listened well. She listened closely to these students now, under the new flag. She bit her lip and tears welled in her eyes. She whispered to Samantha, "I'm overwhelmed."

"Totally." Samantha put her arm over Sarah's shoulder. "Most beautiful thing I've seen."

Sarah recognized Vermont's Secretary of Education, who was offered the mic next. "I want to commend the students, because one of the most important roles of the schools is to help students figure out how to participate in democracy," the official said. "What I appreciate is the fact that they're working to make sure that when we talk about liberty and justice, we're really talking about liberty and justice for all."

After the Montpelier High School event, the months moved quickly in Sarah's work life. During the winter and spring of 2018 she put a lot of miles on her car, meeting with racial justice advocates and activists in Grand Isle and Orleans Counties, near the Canadian border; Windham and Bennington Counties, facing Massachusetts; and every county in between.

In March, Samantha introduced Sarah to the GMBLM board at a meeting in Barre, Montpelier's neighboring town, fittingly held at the Old Labor Hall, built in 1900 by the Italians who had come to Barre to work in the granite mines and sheds as quarry men and stone cutters. Aside from Elena and Chip Skinner, whom she had met at the Sacred Grounds Café during her interview, the board included two student organizers, respectively from Montpelier High School and U-32, a city councilor from Montpelier, and a newly recruited legislator from Norwich, a town an hour southeast on the Interstate.

Some board members congratulated Samantha, Chip, and Elena on what appeared to be a successful hiring process. Others were eager to elicit Sarah's views. What campaigns did she have in mind? Where was the balance between structural change and symbolic success? Did she see curriculum reform as important?

Sarah was deferential on most of these matters. She was too new to the position, she said, and needed to learn more, to visit more schools, meet with the student activists, listen to their concerns. She was pleased, though, to report on significant progress at U-32, the high school that served the towns around Montpelier.

Sarah had been meeting with the U-32 multicultural group going by the name BLAAMM—Blacks, Latinos, Asians, And Many More. BLAAMM had begun a discussion with the school board early in the school year about racism and intolerance. The board was persuaded to approve BLAAMM's request to fly the Black Lives Matter flag on the school's flagpole, just as Montpelier had done. The ceremony was scheduled for June fifth.

Sarah had arrived early to the U-32 campus. The mood was dampened by continuing concerns over the possibility of disruption and violence. The driveway gates were locked well before things got started, and the outdoor area around the flagpole was patrolled by faculty, staff, and a police officer. It felt to her more like a prison yard than a school celebration.

Her mood improved once the event began. A sophomore from Barre was the one who hoisted the flag, unsuccessful at first; the flag was attached to the rope upside down and raised to half-mast before the mistake was noticed, but the flag was dropped down, flipped the right way around, and raised again. No one seemed to mind.

One of the U-32 students Sarah had come to know, a junior, spoke movingly to the assembly gathered at the flagpole. "This flag, to me, represents equality, inclusiveness, and most of all—hope," she said. "Hope that, in the future, not just this school but this nation will learn the beauty of differences and the importance of change. The racism needs to stop, the police brutality needs to stop, the stereotyping needs to stop, but most of all the oppression needs to come to an end."

Not all shared her sentiments. Sarah noticed a younger student holding a banner proclaiming *All Lives Matter*. She went over to talk with him. He told her he was in the seventh grade and that the Black Lives Matter flag was divisive, not inclusive. "I can't support this movement. It's just making us all angry."

A friend of his joined in. "I don't object to most of the stuff they're saying," the friend told her, "but they shouldn't be raising that flag up there. It's not right."

"Why do you think that?" Sarah asked.

"Because they think they're better than us."

The boy holding the banner punched his friend in the arm, grinning. "They *are* better than you."

Sarah smiled and shook her head, moving through the crowd. She found one student leader talking to a group around him. "Everywhere I go," he was saying, "I am described not by the many personality traits that make me who I am, but as a 'black kid' or 'the mixed boy.' I mean, these are the kind of racist, disrespectful, hurtful things minority students endure on a daily basis."

He emphasized that the new banner was not intended to be divisive. "The flag is not meant to take a voice away from any other race, or symbolize that we matter more than everybody else, but that we mean just as much to our school as the majority does and we will be accepted the way we are, without having to alter ourselves to fit in."

With these words in mind, Sarah felt hopeful as she got into her car and drove out of the U-32 parking lot. The school's long driveway came out to the road, where the gate had been unlocked and was swung wide open again. Standing silently at the intersection was a small group of protesters holding signs. Sarah paused in her car and stared.

She first noticed several *Blue Lives Matter* placards. One person held a sign proclaiming *Protect the Second Amendment.* Another sign, more ominous, read *Go Home to Your Own Countries!*

As she pulled out to make the turn, she saw a broad-shouldered man at the edge of the group who held aloft a sign with the words, *White Patriots*, with a swastika below the words. The man glared at her.

Sarah gripped the steering wheel as she tried to focus on getting away without going off the road.

Part II
Patriots

Again, the man wakes Sarah. "I was watching you asleep," he says in his Trump mask. "I brought you another cheese sandwich and some grapes."

Sarah has little idea how much time has gone by. Two days? Three days? The light is the same. There's no window in the bathroom, just light coming through the opening in the door. It appears to be artificial light.

Sarah pulls herself up and looks at the man in the mask. She takes the food from him and asks, "What are you planning to do?"

"Stop the lawsuit."

"How will this help you do that?"

"I'm gonna tell them I'll let you out without hurting you if they stop it. For good."

Sarah thinks this is crazy. Any purported dismissal of the case that is filed under duress will not be effective, she's pretty sure. She wonders if she should tell the man. She decides not to. Instead, she says, "Okay. When will you tell them?"

"Today," he says.

"How will you tell them? Will you use a phone?"

"Don't get me talking about that," he stutters behind the Trump face. "You're clever." He coughs. "Sick of this thing," he complains, referring to his mask.

Aside from everything else about the condition of her life in this moment, Sarah agrees with the man; she finds it unnerving to talk to a mask. She asks, "Where did you find that mask?"

"My brother gave it to me. He thought it was funny."

"Is it hard to breathe when you wear it?"

"Nah," he answers.

"I'm having trouble breathing," says Sarah but then she is not sure if she said this aloud.

"Would you like to have a shower?" the man asks.

This takes her by surprise. "Yes," she answers quickly, but there is no shower in her little bathroom jail cell. "Where can I get a shower?"

"If you promise to do everything like I tell you, I'll bring you to a shower upstairs. After you eat the sandwich."

She thinks he's probably going to watch her. Maybe that's what this is about. Or maybe worse. She feels afraid again.

"I won't hurt you," he says, as if he knows her thoughts. "I won't touch you. You'll need to wear a bag over your head when I bring you to the bathroom upstairs. I'll need to make sure you don't cause trouble, but you can be behind the shower curtain. It'll be okay, Sarah."

He used her name. "What should I call you?" she asks.

"I don't know. I'm not giving you my real name." He ponders while she finishes the sandwich. American cheese on white bread, but she is not complaining. "How about Jack?"

Sarah feels the man is warming to her as a human being. Instinctively she reciprocates and she feels safer. "Okay, Jack, I would like to take a shower. May I please also have a toothbrush and toothpaste?"

He says he'll get her those things later, and hands her a paper bag. She puts it over her head and waits. The door opens, he takes her arm, and she steps out of the cell. She is not wearing shoes. He puts the rubber band around the bag on her head. He guides her up a flight of stairs.

She can tell there is more light here. The air is better. He is touching her arm gently now, and he brings her into a room. He closes the door and the air again is stale. He tells her she can take off the bag. His voice too is gentler now than it was back when he first got into her car, what feels like many weeks ago.

Sarah and the man are in a bathroom with a tub that has a shower curtain. The bathroom is unfinished, with rough lumber and no sheetrock or painted surfaces. There are no windows. When Jack in the mask gestures to the tub, she steps into the tub and draws the curtain closed. She removes her clothing and places it on the floor outside the tub. There is shampoo and soap on the tub's edge.

She turns the water on, standing to the side as best she can until it reaches the right temperature. She wonders if Jack will pull the shower curtain aside. She senses he wants to look at her body. She doesn't really care about that now, and she suds up and down her torso, her legs and arms. She squirts shampoo into her hand, closes her eyes, and massages her scalp.

Her eyes are closed, and she knows the man is on the other side of the shower curtain. She is vulnerable, a naked prisoner woman with an unstable man in a mask a few feet away. She continues to rub the shampoo through her hair as if to erase her desperation. Maybe the man has left the room? She stops rubbing to listen, but the water is drumming down from the shower faucet and she can't hear anything else. But then she thinks she hears a bit of movement from the other side of the curtain. Maybe she hears breathing from behind the mask he wears.

With her eyes closed she decides to focus on Ricky and how they used to take showers together in the tub in her Providence apartment. They lathered each other, all over their bodies. They touched each other—no! she stops the dream.

She cannot, in this place, feel sexual. Her body does not belong to her in this prison. Sarah rinses her hair and opens her eyes. She is still alone in the tub. She rinses the rest of her. She turns the faucet off.

It is quiet and they wait.

"Here," he finally says, handing her a towel around the curtain, careful not to push it aside. "I hope that made you feel better."

On a Thursday morning in late summer, Sarah sat in her kitchen with her coffee and a fried egg with toast. She'd opened her email and scrolled through her inbox.

Ricky sat across the small table from her. His long body was too big for the space. When he worked in it—which was often, as he was the family cook and baker and coffee brewer—it appeared to Sarah he was a circus acrobat practicing complex routines.

He was relaxed now; it was summer break from his tutoring job at the school. He was reading the *Times Argus*. He'd been up early and already had his breakfast and coffee. He would head out momentarily for his morning run.

She buttered her toast, spooned on some apricot preserve, and came upon an email from an unknown source. It said simply:

"WHY ARE YOU A WHITE GIRL HELPING COLOREDS?"

She inhaled audibly and Ricky looked up from the paper.

She turned her laptop to face Ricky across the table.

He read the email. "Oh Sarah," he said, "do you know where it comes from?"

"I have no idea," she said. She'd told him about the opponents to the campaign to fly the BLM flag at U-32, the protestors with their signs. "It's obviously connected to the work we're doing. You know we faced a lot of hostility, some of it pretty racist. Some of them are associated with gun rights. They've been talking about flying a flag of some gun organization."

"You think it's them?"

"It must be. Or somebody connected to them, somebody sympathetic. Who else?" She read it again. "The word *coloreds* is bizarre."

"It creeps me out," said Ricky. "But how is it different from saying *people of color*?"

"Oh Christ, Ricky, it's not the same. Words are fraught with historical meaning. *Colored* takes us back to water fountains and Jim Crow. Not just that," she added, trying not to get irritated and judgmental, "but the concept of questioning why a white person should help people of color is racist."

"I know that, Sarah. But the word's still arbitrary. They're just words and you don't have to weigh them down with the baggage of history. Maybe it just comes out of ignorance. Don't patronize me."

"I'm not the one weighing words down. A history of racism weighs them down. I'm not patronizing you, just telling you like it is."

"Fuck you, too," he said in a collaborative vein, smiling, and Sarah smiled back at him, her forgiving and reasonable partner.

"But what do I do about this fucking email?" she asked him.

"I guess let it go. I wouldn't answer it in any case. Obviously, since there's no one identified to answer to." He got up and came around the table. "Come here," he said. "It'll be all right, Sarah."

Sarah stood and grasped Ricky and held him close. She pulled him into a tight embrace, until she felt him hardening against her. Sarah never tired of his persistent, helpless cock.

"You are so unbearably cute and sexy," he told her.

"Go for your run now, before the temperature hits eighty."

"What will you do about the email?"

"I'll ignore it. Okay?"

"Okay. But save it. Creepy."

Gerald Croome was a partner at Shelby & Croome, P.C., the law firm located in a handsomely refurbished red brick building on Burlington's waterfront. He addressed a letter to the new superintendent of schools of the Washington Central Unified Union School District.

Dear Superintendent Bailey:

Please be advised this firm represents the rights and interests of Second Amendment, Inc., a Virginia non-

profit corporation that supports the rights of gun owners in Vermont and other states (hereafter "2dA"), and
Collin Chapman, through his parents Ernest and Tammie Chapman, residents of Calais, Vermont, and 2dA
members. Collin is presently a ninth grader at U-32
High School.

As you know, the District's decision to permit the
so-called Black Lives Matter flag to be hoisted on
the school campus in June engendered considerable
dissent and charges of partisanship. Collin and other
students who objected to the BLM flag met with Associate Principal Silas Turner on September 4, 2018, to
discuss their concerns. They presented the 2dA flag,
politely requesting that it be flown on the school flagpole either alongside the BLM flag during the period
the BLM flag is flown or consecutively for the same
length of time.

As we understand the facts, Mr. Turner took the students' requests under advisement, though we have no
knowledge at present with whom, if anyone, he sought
advice. One week later, however, Mr. Turner met again
with the students and told them abruptly that the
school district would not honor their request. He gave
them no cogent explanation for his decision.

This was a violation of the dissenting students' First
Amendment rights, including Collin's rights. By permitting the BLM flag to fly on the school's flagpole,
the District created what the law has recognized
as a designated public forum for engaging in free
expression, in which a governmental body is pro-

hibited from discriminating on the basis of the viewpoint of the speaker. That is precisely what the District did in this case. Its action is abhorrent to First
Amendment principles.

Collin has a compelling claim under 42 U.S.C. § 1983
that the District violated his right to free speech under
the First Amendment. 2dA also has a compelling claim,
as an organization that promotes the interests of gun
owners in Vermont, that the District similarly violated
its right to free expression under the First Amendment.
We intend to press both claims.

We are prepared to file suit in federal court. We are
willing, however, to discuss settlement with you prior
to filing suit. Any settlement would require injunctive
relief as well as compensation for damages incurred
by my clients. Please contact me within seven days.

Washington Central's new superintendent, Sherise Bailey,
clenched her teeth, trying to remember exactly which associate
principal Silas Turner was. She'd only recently met the folks at
U-32. She forwarded the emailed letter over to the District's lawyer,
Tadeusz Sorowski, and called him ten minutes later.

"This will require research," said Sorowski, "before I can give
you an informed opinion on the law relevant to this matter. I would
also ask you to prepare for me a chronology of the events relating
to this flag matter, with copies of correspondence and documents
that pertain."

He cleared his throat. "I would have preferred," he went on
in his formal manner, "had you or the board, or your predecessor,
conferred with me earlier in the process."

"I know, Tad. Me too. We weren't expecting a letter from a
lawyer though. Hindsight is wonderful, you know? Stuff happens

and develops its own momentum. And there's been some confusion in view of the administrative transition."

They arranged for a meeting the following day. At the appointed time, Tad Sorowski, attired in his summer-weight suit, appeared at the superintendent's office. Bailey made him feel welcome.

"No coffee, thank you. A glass of cold water, perhaps?" Thus settled, he began his explanation. "The Second Amendment group has raised what is known as the public forum doctrine. A government body—and a public school district of course qualifies as such—may create a forum that is designated for certain types and manners of speech. If it does so, however, it may not discriminate based on the viewpoint expressed by the speaker. What I can advise you is that the District would face legal jeopardy if, indeed, it has created such a limited public forum."

"So, then, Attorney Sorowski," her formality delivered with humor and a hint of irony, "did we create a forum? By allowing BLM to fly their flag?"

"I would argue," Tad answered, "that you have not created a forum for student speech."

"How not?" asked Superintendent Bailey. She pushed her glasses higher on her nose.

"Schools are different," he responded obscurely. "Let me back up a bit. While students do enjoy the right to free speech protected by the First Amendment, at the same time there are limits to the constitutional right that do not generally apply outside of the school context. I believe you are already familiar with the notion that school officials have the authority to restrain speech that substantially disrupts the educational process, what is sometimes called the *Tinker* test. But we would not rely on that doctrine."

"Okay." Patiently.

"We would not rely on it in part because the *Tinker* test does not permit viewpoint discrimination. In any event, it would be difficult, I believe, to make the requisite showing that allowing Second Amendment, the gun rights group, to fly their flag on the school flagpole would be substantially disruptive to school operations when you have already permitted the Black Lives Matter group to fly their flag. You understand? However, there is another doctrine that I believe applies in this context."

"Yes?"

"There is a 1988 decision by the U.S. Supreme Court, called *Hazelwood School District v. Kuhlmeier*. The case involves a high school in Missouri. The school had a journalism class in which students could enroll for credit. In this class, the students wrote, edited, and produced a newspaper. There was a school board policy pertaining to school-sponsored student publications. The policy required that such publications should not restrict diverse viewpoints and should be consistent with the adopted curriculum. You're following?"

"I'm following, Attorney Sorowski." She smiled at him.

"The particular issue that arose in the court case involved a student-written article that described the experiences of three of the school's students who were or had been pregnant, and an article that discussed the impact of divorce on students. Concerns were raised with the school principal as to whether the anonymity of students whose stories were told in the articles was sufficiently protected. Concerns were also expressed about inappropriate sexual content."

Tad paused to make sure the superintendent was with him. "You can presumably understand such concerns."

"Yes, of course," she said.

"The principal then made the decision to delete those pages that contained the articles he considered objectionable. And it was that action of censorship that was eventually upheld by the Supreme Court. That is to say, the court ruled that the First Amendment rights of these students were not violated. Why not?"

Tad peered at Sherise to see if she would offer her opinion.

She did not, and waited him out.

"The court," he went on, "held that the newspaper was not a forum for public expression. You see, that is the key: the newspaper was not considered to be a forum for free speech. Hence, students did not have the right to publish whatever articles they pleased."

"I hear what you're saying," said Bailey, "but I confess I'm not altogether clear why it goes that way. Why *isn't* the student newspaper a forum for free speech?"

"Ah. That raises the precise point at issue. It was not truly a *student* newspaper. I think I can elucidate." Tad then read from the Court opinion. "'School facilities,'" he quoted, "'may be deemed to be public forums only if school authorities have by policy or by practice opened those facilities for indiscriminate use by the general public, or by some segment of the public, such as student organizations. If the facilities have instead been reserved for other intended purposes, communicative or otherwise, then no public forum has been created, and school officials may impose reasonable restrictions on the speech of students, teachers, and other members of the school community.'"

"All right, it's making a bit more sense. No public forum was intended, so no public forum was created?"

"Close," instructed the pedantic lawyer. "Intent may not be required. One might create a public forum by practice, even if unintended, I suppose, so long as the practice is to allow indiscriminate use by a segment of the public."

"All right. How clever you are, Attorney Sorowski," she beamed.

"We may apply the reasoning to the circumstances here at U-32," he went on without pause. "The school flagpole has similarly not been opened up for indiscriminate use by student organizations. In the case of student publications that are sponsored by the school and are a part of the curriculum, or, to take another example, a school's theatrical productions, educators are entitled to exercise editorial control over the content and style of the production.

"This is so in circumstances where, as the Court put it, the expressive activity might reasonably be perceived 'to bear the imprimatur of the school.' The only limitation is this: the school administrator's actions must be 'reasonably related to legitimate pedagogical concerns.'"

"I believe we have legitimate reasons," opined the superintendent. "Does *imprimatur* just mean *approval*?"

"That is a good question," Sorowski said. "I think it is more than approval. The connotation is that the school district has given its official sanction. Or it has in some relevant fashion sponsored the speech at issue. I believe the question we must ask is—whether the board's decision, on the one hand, to permit the school's flagpole to be used to fly the Black Lives Matter flag but, on the other hand, to deny its use for flying the Second Amendment group's flag—whether those decisions are reasonably related to legitimate pedagogical concerns."

Sorowski paused, and asked, "Can you do that? Can you make that showing?"

"I don't see why not," replied the superintendent. "We are trying to teach tolerance, democratic values, respect for everyone, the value of everyone's life and right to enjoy life and to receive a fair education. Our African American students, and our African immigrant students, and people of color in this school, must all be made welcome. That's why we allowed the BLM flag to fly here. You get it."

"I do," replied the lawyer, admiring Sherise, who, as an African American herself, spoke with greater insight on these issues than most. "That indeed sounds like a legitimate pedagogical concern. And the decision to decline to fly the other flag?"

"We do not take a position on the individual right to bear arms," she replied. "I guess I would say we are opposed to permitting free access to weapons—of course, there is board policy prohibiting students from bringing weapons to school—but we express no view on the broader questions. Personally, I have some views about that."

"As do I," said Sorowski.

Alicia Santana was Sam Jacobson's law partner and a long-time friend of the family. Both Sarah and Ricky felt close to her. She'd befriended and helped Ricky during the period in his life when he had sent the infamous homophobic message to his late classmate. Ricky described Alicia as having saved him.

Sarah, too, felt indebted to Alicia for that reason. But there was more: Alicia and her wife, Barb Laval, had for years socialized with the Jacobsons, and on several occasions, as Sarah later remembered (or reconstructed) events, Alicia had gently mediated arguments between the teenaged Sarah and her father. Alicia had the sort of uncanny, sunny intelligence that allowed her to see the best in both sides and to persuade the opposing parties to do so too.

Sarah had called Alicia with her more recent problem. "U-32's been sued," she began, "for flying the Black Lives Matter flag. Or, I guess, more for not flying the flag of this other student group that wants more freedom for gun owners."

Alicia knew about Sarah's new job. "Is Tad Sorowski representing the school district?" was her first question.

"Yes, that's what I heard."

"That's good; he's good, very capable," Alicia said. She knew Tad fairly well and admired him, in spite of his pretensions, having been on opposite sides in some contentious cases. "Who's the plaintiff and who represents them?"

"There's a group of students and their parents too, called Second Amendment. I don't really know who they are, maybe just an *ad hoc* group formed in opposition to BLM."

"Who do they have as a lawyer?"

"It's some Burlington firm. I don't know."

"Where's it filed?" was Alicia's next question. Alicia's intellectual energy was relentless once she got going. Sarah imagined Alicia on the phone at her desk, leaning forward, furiously taking notes.

"Federal court," Sarah answered.

"Makes sense," said Alicia, "if they're raising a First Amendment challenge. What do you need, Sarah?"

"I'm wondering if we should be involved in the lawsuit."

"By *we*, you mean . . . ?"

"Green Mountain BLM."

"But you haven't been sued yourselves, right?" asked the lawyer.

"No."

"Have you talked it through with Samantha Janey?"

"Yeah, she knows I'm calling you. The board too."

The phone was quiet for a moment. "It's possible, I suppose, for Green Mountain BLM to intervene, or to participate as an *amicus* party, a friend of the court. The organization's interests, I think we could argue, are also at stake here. Hey Sam," Sarah could hear Alicia yell, "it's Sarahkins on the phone!"

Alicia was the only person other than her father who could call her that. "That's it, Alicia. That's kind of why I called. To see if you might be interested in representing us in that way. So, is my pops there?"

"He is; he's grumbling his way over to my office. Do you have a copy of the complaint you can get me?"

"No."

"That's okay. I'll ask Tad to send me one. I'll be happy to look at it and think about it. Does Sam know about this yet?"

"Yes, about the case, but not about us getting involved in it."

"Hello, Sarah?" Sam had grabbed Alicia's phone. "What's all this about? Everything all right?"

"Everything's fine, Dad. Alicia will tell you, okay? I've got to get back to work."

Sam handed the phone back to Alicia, who said, "Okay, hon, let me look into it a bit. I've got to understand the issues and the legal theories before I commit to doing more. I guess we're talking *pro bono*, right?"

Even when he'd lived in New York and Providence, Ricky jogged regularly. Running on city streets with noise and traffic was an entirely different sort of running than his new rural running routine in Vermont. He was a man of habits; if he liked a way of doing things, he kept doing it that way. If he grew to like a particular route, he stuck with it.

His normal route from his door on downtown Sproul Street brought him straight up North Street, which climbed high into East Montpelier and turned to gravel between farm pastures with western views of the Abenaki Range; then right on Goodman Road past cornfields and into the quiet woods; another right onto County Road, pavement again, pounding back down, crossing Turley Crescent into Montpelier.

It hurt.

He did it anyway, three or four times a week. He liked it even in the heat, though it wouldn't be so hot on this particular Saturday morning in early October. He liked to sweat. He told Sarah he was sweating his demons out.

Ready to run, he opened the apartment door, and an envelope fell to the floor. It wasn't marked. He stood there in the doorway in his shorts and sneakers, and opened the envelope. A typed message:

Sarah Jacobson –

I hate you for working for all the colored people trying to replace the American flag. We got enough problems in America. Stop coming to the school. Your not wanted. If you don't go we'll make sure you do.

From true patriots

Ricky sank down to his haunches, his mind swirling. Sarah was out on the road for meetings with student organizers in Brattleboro, two hours south on the highway. She wouldn't be back for several hours.

He placed the paper back in the envelope and tucked it into his book bag hanging on a hook behind the front door. He didn't want Sarah to come upon it just lying there if she got home before he did. He needed desperately to talk with her about this letter, but he also wanted it to disappear.

How, he wondered, could he protect her from hatred? For a moment he mused on the wisdom of keeping secrets to protect a person you love.

He went on his run up North Street, sweating and still worrying.

Much later that day—Ricky was long since home and had done the dishes from breakfast and put a load of laundry in the washing machine and eaten some carrot sticks and hummus and read two more of the Ta-Nehisi Coates essays from the volume Sarah had given him for his birthday, and then had hung the wet clean clothes on the drying rack they kept in the living room and then showered and prepared a baked rice curry dish with sweet potatoes and raisins—much later, Sarah came home from her road trip to Brattleboro.

She found him on the tiny balcony at the back of the apartment, with a beer in his hand, a beer called Sip of Sunshine. "Happy to see you, Sarah sweetie. How did it go? You want one?" nodding to the beer.

"Sure, let me go put this stuff down and pee and I'll be right out. Can we sit out here for a bit?" It was such a pleasant evening, the sun now in the west, lighting up the parking lot behind the building, the evening still warm enough to sit out on the balcony.

Ricky brought out another Sip of Sunshine and the envelope, sat in one of the faded beach chairs, and put his feet up on the balcony railing. Sarah came out a moment later, sat with a contented sigh in the companion beach chair, and put her hand on Ricky's curly head. "Mmm, you smell like you just showered."

He handed her the ale. "Yuh, that's true. How was the drive?" he asked. "How'd it go, down in Brattleboro?"

"Pretty good. It's an amazing group of students, very conscious of the issues. There's sort of a student revolt against the social studies teachers because they're not incorporating racial and ethnic perspectives. So, I got to talk about that and help strategize. Good stuff. Long drive though. Hey, what you got there?"

Ricky passed her the envelope. "Take a look." He ground his teeth.

Sarah saw the muscles of his jaw working, familiar to her when he was worrying. She read the note, a frown clouding her face. "What, where . . . ?"

"I found it this morning just by the front door," he explained. "I have no idea where it came from."

"It's so weird," she said.

"I guess," Ricky said. "But then, not a surprise, maybe? It's what you might expect. This is the country we live in now, Sarah. It's Trumpworld."

"Trump didn't create this. It was there all along."

"Maybe so, Sarah. But he overturned the rocks. Remember I told you about that guy I saw at the SURJ meeting I went to, back in the spring? He'd met someone from Burlington who had been marching with the white supremacists in Charlottesville. *Good people on both sides*, according to our president."

"Yeah, I remember you telling me about the conversation at SURJ. I remember the footage of the event in Charlottesville. Those guys screaming *Jews will not replace us*. It's sickening." Sarah sighed again, this time without pleasure. "But I didn't expect it here. In Vermont."

They sat for a while in silence.

"I'm really sorry, Sarah. I almost didn't show it to you. You know?"

"You had to. I have to know what's going on. Jesus."

"Yuh," he said. "I had to. Take it to the police?"

"No, come on, it's just some moron, a kid."

"Right," said Ricky, "a kid moron threatening to hurt you. A kid who's really into guns."

"I'll talk to Alicia Santana about it," she said.

"How is Alicia going to keep you safe?" he asked, not expecting an answer.

The lawyer, Tad Sorowski, had gotten a letter too.

It was mailed to him and he found it in the mailbox when he came home from work one evening. He lived with a woman in a small house on the dirt road that runs between Maple Corner and Worcester, a few miles from Montpelier. The woman was Charlene Nelson, an acupuncturist and herbal healer. Tad called her Charlie, and they'd lived together for thirty years, unmarried, seeing no reason to marry. Odd, this couple, given Tad's pedantic rationalism.

The letter had no return address. He brought it in with the mail, put the junk in the recycle bin, and opened the envelope. He read:

> Mr Sorowski,
>
> Your a dirty jew lawyer and you shouldn't work for the black lives flag people! We know what to do with people like you. Garbage people.
>
> True Patriots

Tad had come to the U.S. from Poland as a young teenager. In fact, he was not Jewish; his parents were Catholic, although his father, a dissident poet as a young man, had been imprisoned in the Auschwitz extermination camp. His father had been demoted to the status of a Jew in 1940s Poland, and now, so was Tad, the seventy-four-year-old son, in 2018 America.

Tad sat quietly with the letter in his hand, thinking about his father, a heavy stone in his gut. His Charlie would be home soon. He would show her the letter, and she would share the weight of the stone.

Alicia invited Tad Sorowski to her office on Chamber Street. It was late afternoon and dusk was approaching. Work was done for the day; this was a chance to let down and talk shop. Alicia offered wine and poured a glass of Pinot Noir for each of them. They sat down in the front conference room, the big window overlooking the downtown street.

Alicia held up her glass and swirled the dark liquid. "I don't think *Hazelwood* is the right precedent here. That was a school-sponsored newspaper, but it was still *student* speech that was involved. We don't have student speech here, really. I think this should be analyzed as the school being the speaker."

"Interesting," said the stiff lawyer.

"You familiar with the *Summum* case, Tad?"

Tad made a non-committal gesture.

"It's *Pleasant Grove City v. Summum*, a 2009 Supreme Court case. This religious organization wanted to erect a monument in a city park that already had a bunch of other monuments. The monument was supposed to have the religion's tenets engraved on it, what they called the Seven Aphorisms of Summum. The city didn't want the group's monument in their park. So, the question is whether the city was required by the Constitution to let the Summum people erect their monument, alongside the other monuments."

"Ah," said Tad. "As in whether the U-32 school district is required to let the Second Amendment people hoist their flag."

"You got it," said Alicia, with a nod. "You're a quick study. Now, the park had a dozen or so other permanent monument-type displays, most of which had been donated to the city by private parties. So, Tad, for example, the park already had a wishing well, a 9/11 monument, a monument of an historic granary, one that represented the city's first fire station, a Ten Commandments monument, and so on. You get the picture."

Tad Sorowski nodded. He got the picture.

"And, of course, the Summum people, the plaintiff, argued the city had created a *forum* for private speech in the form of monuments. Their position was that the city was not allowed to decide—on the basis of who the speaker was and what the content of the message was—which monuments could be erected, and which could not be. They argued, therefore, that the First Amendment *required* the city to display the Summum monument."

"I see," said Tad.

"But the court said no." She smiled at Tad.

"Good," he said.

"The court decided," Alicia went on, "it was the city itself that was engaging in expressive conduct even when accepting monuments donated by private groups. Right? Summum was not the speaker. The fire station people were not the speakers. The Ten Commandments folks were not the speakers, for First Amendment purposes. The *government* was the speaker in all these cases. Why?"

"That is indeed the question. Why?" He sipped the Pinot slowly.

"Because, the court reasoned, the public who used the city park, knowing it was a public park, interpreted the monuments as conveying the city's *own* messages."

"Ah," said Tad.

Alicia moved forward at her usual fast pace, leg bouncing, smiling, tying the knots of the argument. "The U-32 flagpole is like the Pleasant Grove City park. It has room for only so many flags. The individual flags are the individual monuments. When U-32 flies a flag, it is U-32 itself that is expressing its views. The public who sees the flags correctly understands that it is the school district making a point, conveying a message. The flagpole has not become a public forum, limited or otherwise."

"Ah-hah."

They heard a siren outside, and they went to the window. One firetruck was quickly followed by several other emergency vehicles, sirens screaming and lights flashing, racing west on Chambers Street out of sight.

"I wonder where the trucks are headed. Let's hope no one is hurt, Alicia."

"Amen to that." They sat back down. "Where were we?" asked Alicia. "Another glass, Tad? Half? Okay. We were talking about *Summum* and the Pleasant Grove park. Now, *Hazelwood* required that censorship of a school-sponsored student newspaper must be reasonably related to legitimate pedagogical concerns. You don't even need to meet that test here, as easy as it might be.

"U-32 can decline anyone's request to fly their flag, without any special pedagogical justification, because the school has not created any sort of public forum on its flagpole. Which is not to say the school shouldn't have good reasons for any decisions it makes about these kinds of issues. That's a matter of politics, not law."

"Yes, perhaps."

"And there's another, more recent case, Tad, from 2015. Very strange license plate case. *Walker v. Sons of Confederate Veterans.* It takes off from *Summum.*"

"That one I am not familiar with."

"Here's the deal. Car owners in Texas have a choice between ordinary and specialty license plates, all right? A nonprofit can seek to sponsor a specialty plate and may submit a draft design. If the Texas DMV—the Department of Motor Vehicles—approves the design, you can get a specialty plate with that design and put it on your car.

"Now, this group called the Sons of Confederate Veterans proposed a license plate design featuring, not surprisingly, a Confederate battle flag, and they sought approval from the DMV. Had to happen sooner or later." Alicia grinned at her colleague. "But lo and behold, the Texas DMV rejected it."

"Ah," said Tad again.

"The DMV found that much of the public associates the Confederate flag with organizations advocating hate. That seems like an historically fair assessment. But it does raise the question whether a state agency like the DMV can reject a private group's effort to engage in free expression based on the specific content and viewpoint of the expression. In other words, censorship."

"Yes."

"The court ended up saying this was not unconstitutional censorship. And it's because, like *Summum*, the court held that the design and the words on the plate were the speech of the government, the State of Texas, not the private group. And the *government* is entitled to promote a program or push a policy or take whatever position it wishes to."

"Yes, I see," Tad said. "But perhaps it is a stretch to think that those messages on the specialty plates are truly government messages."

"Tad, here's how the court handled it. The court reasoned that license plates and license plate designs are closely identified by the public with the state. The state controls the message. Like, for example, the Texas DMV can offer a license plate that says *Fight Terrorism*. But it doesn't have to offer a plate that promotes ISIS."

"Surely."

Alicia plowed on. "To bring this back to the First Amendment analysis, what this all means is that the Texas specialty plates are not considered a public forum of any kind. Same thing here at our local school. The U-32 flagpole is the license plate. Right? It is not a public forum. The BLM flag is an example of the *school* promoting its *own* message. The Second Amendment group is like the Sons of Confederate Veterans. Probably in more ways than one." She smiled again, inviting solidarity.

Tad nodded that he understood her meaning.

"They have," Alicia continued, "a right to speak freely in all sorts of venues, but they can't appropriate the school's flagpole for their message."

"Very well," said Tad. "Very helpful analysis."

"Another refill?"

Tad put his hand over the wine glass. "Thank you, Alicia, but no. Please have one yourself." She did.

Alicia was not quite finished. "A cautionary note? *Walker v. Confederate Veterans* was five to four. It could easily have gone the other way. Alito dissented with Roberts, Scalia and Kennedy joining. They make fun of the majority. Here's what Alito wrote: 'Suppose you sat by the side of a Texas highway'—sounds like a Jackson Browne song—'and studied the license plates on the vehicles passing by . . . If a car with a plate that says "Rather Be Golfing" passed by at 8:30 a.m. on a Monday morning, would you think: "This is the official policy of the State—better to golf than to work?"' Oh, he's having a good time."

"Jackson who? What is Justice Alito saying?" asked Tad.

"Jackson Browne, but that wasn't Alito; that was just me interjecting. Never mind about that. Alito said that the State of Texas had offered space on its specialty plates like 'little mobile billboards on which motorists can display their own messages.' He called the majority's decision blatant viewpoint discrimination. But hey, that's the minority opinion and it doesn't count."

Sorowski nodded agreement and asked, "Is it clear to you, Alicia, that these cases, *Summum* and this Texas case, apply in the public-school context?"

"I think so. Why not? The doctrine is obviously not limited to monuments in parks, as we know it applies to the totally different context of car license plates. It seems to be far reaching and I can't see why it wouldn't apply to the facts here."

Tad leaned back and studied the ceiling for a few seconds. "We could, I think, argue the doctrines of *Summum* and *Hazelwood* in the alternative. This case could be decided in favor of the school under either theory."

"I agree," said Alicia. "Come to think, the court might stay with *Hazelwood* because then I think it doesn't need to decide precisely who is the speaker, the school or the students. That would be a narrower decision. Like, *even if* the flying of the flag constitutes student speech, it does not follow that the Second Amendment group gets to put its own flag up. The flagpole is not a public forum under either theory.

"Under *Hazelwood*, the school gets to decide which expressive act it will allow, so long as it can show its decision is reasonably related to legitimate pedagogical concerns, or whatever the exact language is."

"You stated it perfectly, Alicia." Tad hesitated for a moment. "What if—" he asked, "—what if it all was the other way 'round?"

"The other way 'round?" she asked.

"Yes, I was not clear," Tad said. "I mean to pose this question: What if the school had endorsed the flag of the gun-rights people, and the BLM people were denied the opportunity to fly their flag? Would we, you and I, Alicia, argue this was unlawful viewpoint discrimination? Would we bring suit under the First Amendment?"

Alicia decided she loved this old man, his pompous eccentricities aside. "That is the question, isn't it, Tad? Do our principles hold?"

"I will surely need to be prepared to answer that question."

Alicia got up and brought the glasses to the sink. "Anything for you, Tad?"

"No, thank you." He then spoke carefully. "Now I wish to tell you something that will change the mood. I am sorry. I have received a strange threatening letter."

"What?"

"A letter, perhaps from the Second Amendment group, but I do not really know, insulting me and, I believe, threatening me, in connection with this case. The writer makes an erroneous assumption that I am Jewish."

"Oh, Tad, I am so sorry!" She reached out to touch his arm. "Sarah Jacobson got letters like that too. Did you know?"

Tad shook his head. "I did not know."

"She showed them to me. With yours added, it all makes me terribly nervous. Will you make me a copy of what they sent you?"

Manny Cruz was in his senior year at Montpelier High School. He had been one of the more outspoken BLM activists behind the campaign to fly the flag the previous year. His parents had immigrated from El Salvador twenty years ago, with Manny's older brother, then a toddler, in tow. Manny had been born in Hartford, Connecticut.

The email he got said:

> You spic Manny. You make me sick. Go home to Mexico.

> Patriots rise!

When the family sat down for dinner that evening, Manny showed his parents the email on his phone. Manny's mother immediately teared up and she rushed from the table. His father grabbed Manny's shoulders. "Where did this come from!" He almost yelled this at his son.

"I have no idea, Dad."

When, a few days later, Sarah opened an email addressed to her that called her a "jewish cunt" and threatened to stop her efforts "by any means," she and Alicia Santana grew more alarmed, assembled their pieces of evidence—though without the email sent to Manny Cruz, of which they remained ignorant—and paid a visit to Montpelier police detective Barry LaPorte.

They asked for Detective LaPorte because Alicia knew him. He was married to Alicia's close friend, Francine Loughlin, who had attended law school with Alicia some twenty years earlier. It was a second marriage for both Barry and Francine.

Alicia trusted Barry completely. He was a hero in her eyes, for he had swept in to take care of Francine when her seventeen-year-old daughter had died in a tragic accident a few years before. Francine's heart had cracked, and it was Barry LaPorte who had helped her mend it.

Barry invited them to his small office at the station. He hugged Alicia, shook Sarah's hand as she introduced herself, grabbed a third chair from a neighboring office, and bid his guests to sit. The visitors declined an offer of coffee.

Barry was large and stoic, and appeared somewhat disheveled and casual for a policeman, dressed in civilian clothes, his hair a rambling gray mess. Yet he conveyed a sense of competence and reliability.

"Long time," he said. "I'm always glad to see you, Alicia."

"I know, Barry, it's been too long. Last time Barb and I visited with you and Frannie, I think, was in the spring, maybe a year and a half ago? You guys came up to our place and Barb had made a huge pot of lentil chili with pork sausage that our neighbor had given us, made from his own pigs. You were suspicious of the sausage. Unreasonably suspicious, I thought." She was, of course, smiling.

She added, "On the other hand, this was the same neighbor who'd painted TAKE BACK VERMONT in huge letters on his barn. So maybe you had good reason to be suspicious. That was before Barb and I moved in."

"Oh, I remember those days," he said. "Now folks have got different fish to fry. You all taught us straights we have nothing to be afraid of. For that, and for your courage, I thank you. And that dinner at your place up there, I remember that too. We had a good time. The sausage was good. I was glad to get Frannie a bit drunk too. You served us Barr Hill gin and tonics, if I recall right. That's good stuff."

He turned in his seat to say, "And pleased to meet you, Sarah. I know your partner, Ricky, and your dad. Good folks. What's up?"

Alicia deferred to Sarah, who handed Barry a copy of the letters and emails. "These started coming a month ago." She explained quickly about the flag campaign, its detractors, and the litigation. He already knew about the tensions and security issues at the school flag-raising events.

Barry read what Sarah handed him. "Oh shit," he summarized. "More darkness. How does Vermont generate so much darkness?" It was a rhetorical question, and no one offered an answer. He then asked a few non-rhetorical questions and took notes. "Let me get on this. You let me know if anything else comes your way."

It was unseasonably warm the next Saturday morning, high fifties anyway. Sarah and Ricky took a bike ride, starting out while it was still misty along the Scape River. Traffic on Route 2 was light, allowing them to ride side by side for parts of the way, as the road hugged the north side of the river, climbing here and there between bedrock ledges.

For the most part they had compatible paces. Though sometimes, annoyingly, Ricky pulled ahead singing an inverted Springsteen lyric to her: "If you should fall behind, I'll wait for you."

"Look at how you can see deep through the woods along here," called out Ricky at one moment. "See the birches?" In the woods the birches stood out, gleaming creamy white. "Such a beautiful time of year," he said.

What time of year wasn't beautiful to Ricky's eyes? He was more tuned in to the seasons than Sarah, more tuned in to nature itself, to the magnificent landscape unfolding around them.

She could pedal along, drafting press releases in her head, thinking through strategies, crafting arguments to defeat pretend adversaries, oblivious to the copious natural world surrounding her. She was like her father, a head full of ideas and argument. Ricky could let that all go and engage fully in the world outside his head. He had all the Zen. It was one of their biggest differences.

They fell into single file as cars passed them. Sarah pedaled in a relatively low gear, her legs churning fast, her cycling shoes clipped to the pedals, pumping up and down, smooth and comfortable.

Ricky, behind her, engaged a higher gear. He cranked slowly as he admired the plants, the rocks, the slope down to the river.

As they rode into the village of Middlesex, Ricky came back up next to Sarah and said, "These letters are making me sick, Sarah."

She nodded and thought, what happened to his Zen?

They turned left to cross the bridge onto Route 100B and headed southerly toward Moretown, starting with a modest climb past the little school called Stone Path Academy on the left and riding stables on the right. The cooler mist stayed below them, and they began happily to sweat. They both liked to sweat; they had that in common.

Sarah dropped to a lower gear for the hill.

Ricky asked, "How are you dealing with them, Sarah?"

"I'm dealing fine," she panted. "I'm not too worried, Ricky. Especially now that we've talked with Barry LaPorte." She was breathing hard. "It's nothing. It's probably an angry kid."

This too was a big difference, she thought, Ricky worried about her. She, on the other hand, remained largely oblivious, both to the natural world's manifold gifts to her senses and to the human world's manifold threats to her safety.

Then she remembered the fear she had felt when she drove past the right-wing demonstrators at U-32 after the BLM flag was raised. Don't fool yourself, she thought.

As she pedaled next to the sparkling Mad River, Sarah continued a catalog of their similarities and differences. Ricky: notices nature, loves nature. Me: not so much. Ricky: pedals slowly at a high ratio. Me: pedal quickly at a low ratio. Ricky: likes to sweat. Me: like to sweat, yay! Ricky: sensitive and thoughtful. Me: selfish and self-centered? Ricky: prefers *Tintin* comics to *Asterix the Gaul*. Me: the other way round.

Sarah had introduced Ricky to these two French comic series. He didn't grow up reading that sort of thing. What did he read as a kid? She chided herself for not knowing.

Annoyed with herself, she happened to glance at the river, and the sun bounced off the water, blinding her for a split second. Sight returned and she suddenly realized that Ricky would never make such a mental list, would never try to analyze their relationship this way. Why did she do it? Was she condemned to make comparisons?

She pedaled forward, looking straight ahead, afraid to turn her head to the Mad River lest it scald her with another flash of uncomfortable brilliance. She opened up the mental catalog again. Am I really self-centered? she asked. Yes, dammit. Ricky: open and inquisitive. Me: judgmental. Yes, dammit, judgmental too.

Ricky: overly anxious about those damned letters and emails. Me: underly-anxious about same. Then she thought about Bernie Sanders, hands waving in the air, growling hoarsely, "enough about her damn emails," when challenged at a presidential debate about the faux scandal of Hillary Clinton's sloppy email practices.

Sarah got pissed off, yet again, about the election, the pandering to Russia, the sheer awfulness of pussy-grabbing Trump, the renascent fascism.

Ricky passed her up the long hill, in some ridiculously high gear. She heard him chant, "If you should fall behind . . ."

They cruised down the south side of the hill, and she caught up to him as he glided where the road leveled off and then wound gently through pastures with the Mad River now glistening on the left.

She knew he had noticed her dark mood, and he left it alone. Here and there, Ricky pointed out the corn husks, grazing heifers, a fallen limb, a cemetery with only three old gravestones, a lichen-covered granite ledge, a hawk, a dead woodchuck, his desperate fear for the well-being of his most precious Sarah.

How lovely is life with Ricky, thought Sarah. How lucky am I. Should I fall behind, he'll wait for me.

❖   ❖   ❖

Tad Sorowski, on behalf of his client, the Washington Central Unified Union School District, filed a motion to dismiss the complaint of Second Amendment for failure to state a claim. The premise of a motion to dismiss of this type is simple: assuming all the facts pleaded by the plaintiff are true, and even bending all inferences from the alleged facts in the plaintiff's favor, the legal theories brought by the plaintiff must be rejected nonetheless because, as a matter of law, the assumed-to-be-true facts fail to support a valid legal claim.

That is what Tad argued in his memorandum filed with the court in support of the motion. And that is what Alicia argued in her supporting memorandum for the intervenor party, Green Mountain BLM.

Once Gerald Croome, on behalf of his clients, Collin Chapman and Second Amendment, Inc., filed his response, federal Judge Mildred Wallis scheduled a hearing on the motion to dismiss. The hearing was in November at the Fred I. Parker Federal Courthouse in Burlington.

Judge Wallis first addressed Gerald Croome. "You argue the law is in your clients' favor. I'd like you to address the precedents cited by the school board. Tell me why you think they don't apply."

Alicia respected Judge Wallis and had often appreciated her acerbic comments. Aging and overweight, the judge was known by Vermont lawyers to be exceptionally able.

Gerald Croome, at the plaintiffs' table facing the bench, stood up in his pinstripe suit. Another lawyer and a paralegal from his firm sat to his right, and his young client, Collin Chapman, was on his left. The boy's parents, Ernest and Tammie Chapman, sat behind them.

"Certainly, your honor," Croome said. "Let me start with *Hazelwood v. Kuhlmeier*. School officials may, under the law as laid out in that case, suppress student articles in a school-sponsored newspaper for legitimate reasons, such as limiting the content to age-appropriate discussions relating to matters of sex. Or they may stop publication of an article if the article is likely to disclose private matters that an individual might wish to keep confidential.

"That is what *Hazelwood* stands for, your honor. It does not stand for the proposition that a school official may censor a student-written article based on the political viewpoint expressed by the student or based on the political viewpoints of the school administrators. That is what is happening in the present case of the flags. The school administration has decided, based on its own liberal views, that liberal students may fly a Black Lives Matter flag on the school's flagpole, but that conservative students are not permitted to fly the Second Amendment flag that better represents their own views."

The lawyer paused to look down at Collin Chapman, who was biting his nails in the chair next to him. "You cannot sugar-coat this, your honor. It is pure discrimination based on political viewpoint. This has nothing to do with legitimate pedagogical concerns.

"Frankly, we don't think the administration should have allowed the Black Lives flag to be flown in the first place. The flagpole is not the place for this sort of advocacy. But once they made that choice, ill-advised as it was—once they allowed one advocacy group to appropriate the flagpole for its message—they cannot then turn around and turn away another advocacy group, which happens to have a conservative message that is not deemed to be politically correct. This is anathema to core First Amendment principles."

Attorney Croome knows his stuff, thought Alicia. She, Sarah Jacobson, and Samantha Janey were seated at a table behind the main defendant's table, where Tad Sorowski sat alongside Superintendent Sherise Bailey and Board Chair Allen Dahlbert, all facing the raised bench.

"Suppose," challenged Judge Wallis, "one of these students in the journalism class writes an article or an opinion piece in favor of white supremacy. Let's say it's in favor of Nazi ideology. Are you telling me the school administration is prohibited from taking any action about that? They have to publish it in the school newspaper? They have no editorial control?"

"That's a very extreme example," said Croome.

"Which is why I want you to answer it," the judge replied.

"Then no," said Croome, "the school administrators are not permitted to censor the articles based on political viewpoint. They can still apply the *Tinker* test if the material will end up causing disruption to regular school operations. But once they create this kind of limited forum for speech, for editorials in a newspaper, they can't choose to showcase just the liberal views."

"The consequence of your position may be that schools simply cancel their journalism classes. Not a result we should favor, I would think," said the judge. "Also, not a result that promotes the values of the First Amendment."

"I am not in favor of that result either, your honor," Croome went on. "We argue that school newspapers at the high school level should allow a broad range of opinion to be expressed by the class participants. Opinions that reflect the diverse views of American society."

"You're telling us," the judge said, "that if one student writes a piece sympathetic to civil rights or Martin Luther King, say, or, let's go back a bit in history, a piece admiring Abraham Lincoln, then the school must allow a student to publish a piece, in the school-sponsored newspaper, advocating the pro-slavery position?"

"Judge, the First Amendment doesn't play favorites."

"All right," said the judge to Croome. "What about the *Summum* line of reasoning?"

"*Summum*, your honor, was based on the assumption that passersby—that the public—would be likely to reach a conclusion that the park monuments expressed the views of the city itself. Based on that assumption, the court held that no public forum had been created with respect to monuments. We don't think the same can be said here.

"People who view the Black Lives Matter flag, especially people who are familiar with the press coverage of these events, know perfectly well that it is the students who are behind this effort. That is to say, it is a certain group of students, not all of them—it is the students who wish to express a message, I suppose, of some kind of solidarity with African Americans, however misguided.

"Let me just say, your honor, at the minimum there is a factual question here on this precise topic about who really is the speaker here. To try to decide this question on a motion to dismiss would be premature."

"Thank you, Mr. Croome. Mr. Sorowski, how do you respond?"

"Ah, thank you, your honor." Tad Sorowski stood, buttoning his jacket in his usual manner. "On the last point, I believe the question of how the public reasonably interprets a message is not the sort of factual question that requires an evidentiary hearing. To the contrary, I believe it might better be characterized as a legal question, or perhaps a mixed question of law and fact, that the court may decide up front.

"Hence, for example, in *Summum*, the Supreme Court did not appear to rely upon evidence or findings regarding how persons would view the park monuments. The court, rather, ruled on its own that a reasonable person using the park would perceive the monuments as expressing the views of the city rather than as expressing the views of the groups who donated the funds to erect particular monuments.

"Likewise, in the Texas license plate case, your honor, cited in our papers, the Supreme Court reached the legal conclusion, again apparently without an evidentiary record, that the reasonable observer would understand that the vehicle license plate conveyed a message of the State of Texas, rather than a message issued by the owner of the vehicle. To bring this back to the present case, your honor, there is no dispute that the flagpole is school property and that it has never been opened up as a forum for use by the general public or by student groups."

"Well," interrupted the judge, "you may be begging the question on your last point. The question indeed is whether the school board has created at least a limited public forum for student groups to use the school's flagpole to express their views."

"We contend it has not, your honor."

"I know that's your contention, Mr. Sorowski."

"Yes, your honor. The same question was raised in *Summum* and *Walker*. Did Pleasant Grove City create a limited public forum for local organizations or wealthy patrons to engage in expressive conduct by way of erecting monuments of various sorts in the city park? Did the Texas motor vehicles department create a limited public forum for Texas drivers to engage in expressive conduct by purchasing specialty license plates with their own personal messages?

"The answer, in both cases, is no; no public forum of any kind was created. As a matter of law, based on what the reasonable observer understands, the monuments express the views of Pleasant Grove City. The specialty plates express the views of the State of Texas. Perhaps, your honor, one might find the reasoning in the Texas case attenuated." Tad cleared his throat. "One might find it implausible to believe that a license plate proclaiming *I'd rather be golfing* is in fact the speech of the State of Texas, as the dissenting justices devilishly pointed out.

"If that is true, I can only say that the case before you today does not suffer from such infirmities. There is nothing whatsoever implausible in the proposition that the school's flagpole belongs to the school and that the flags hoisted thereupon represent the institution's messages."

"No, the school is not likely," surmised the judge, "to fly a flag that states *I'd rather be golfing*."

"Precisely, your honor."

"Why can't the school install several flagpoles and fly a variety of flags?" pursued the judge.

"It can," said Sorowski. He hadn't thought much about this possibility. "It can, but it need not. And if it did, then it would still have the authority to decide what message its multiple flags ought to convey."

Tad stopped talking but did not sit down. He reviewed his notes. "May I address the points arising under *Hazelwood v. Kuhlmeier*, your honor?"

"You may," said Judge Wallis.

"The school is a special place in First Amendment jurisprudence. In *Hazelwood*, the Supreme Court held that school officials have the authority to regulate school-sponsored expressive activities, such as publications, newspapers, and theatrical productions, if those activities are related to the school's curriculum and if the school officials' decisions are reasonably related to legitimate pedagogical concerns.

"The way the court characterized it is that the First Amendment rights of the student are much more limited in cases where the speech bears the imprimatur of the school—unlike, for example, Mr. Tinker's unimpeded choice to express his opposition to the war in Vietnam by wearing a black armband. Thus, in *Hazelwood*, the principal properly exercised editorial control over a school-sponsored student newspaper."

"But in *Hazelwood*," the judge interrupted, "the suppression of speech was based, as I understand it, on legitimate concerns unrelated to the *viewpoints* of the student speakers. Would you address Mr. Croome's argument about the school discriminating among speakers based on their political opinions?"

"Certainly. Once the government creates a public forum, it may not discriminate on the basis of the speaker's viewpoint. We agree with that proposition. But under *Hazelwood*, no public forum of any kind was created by the school when it agreed to publish a newspaper as part of a journalism class, part of the curriculum.

"Specifically, what the Court held," Sorowski read from the opinion, "is that 'school facilities may be deemed to be public forums only if school authorities have by policy or by practice opened those facilities for indiscriminate use by the general public, or by some segment of the public, such as student organizations. If the facilities have instead been reserved for other intended purposes, communicative or otherwise, then no public forum has been created, and school officials may impose reasonable restrictions on the speech of students, teachers, and other members of the school community.' That's at 484 U.S. page 266."

"*Reasonable* restrictions," interrupted the judge again. "The question remains, Mr. Sorowski, whether it is reasonable to allow one student group's preferred flag on the school's flagpole but not another's, when the distinction appears to be grounded in the political opinions of the two groups."

"I understand, your honor, and the answer is yes. Unequivocal yes. The school administration has the right and authority to decide what messages it wants to convey in a nonpublic forum. Neither of the two groups has the *right* to fly a flag on the school's mast or otherwise to have the school endorse or sponsor its message. That is a choice for the school to make. Of course, on the other side of the coin, students in *both* groups do have the right to speak in school about the issues they care about and to wear buttons, for example, or even hold signs at appropriate gatherings, displaying a political message."

The judge held up a hand and stopped him. "We are in Vermont, Mr. Sorowski. Suppose we were in Mississippi. I don't wish to stereotype Mississippi, but let's get real. Suppose a school there decides to display a Confederate flag on the school flagpole, and a group of students and parents objects. The logic of your position holds that you would concede to the school administration in my hypothetical."

Sorowski frowned and considered. This was a variation on the question he had discussed with Alicia. "Yes, that is so. I would concede on the constitutional argument."

The concession hung in the air for a moment. Then the lawyer spoke slowly. "I would, on the other hand, support the students and parents in protesting the school administration's decision."

"Ah, have your cake and eat it too?"

"No, not that, your honor. Constitutional law and politics are separable. They are distinct fields." He offered up an ironic smile, which the judge returned. "Let me suggest—aside from the controversy surrounding this issue—there is nothing surprising about the concept that the school administration gets to select the messages it wants to convey and, by doing so, it is not depriving those with opposing views of their First Amendment rights. Every policy adopted by the school board is an example of the school's own speech."

"What do you mean by that?"

"Let me illustrate with an example, your honor. The board has, in fact, adopted a policy entitled *Co-Curricular Equity and Access*, which includes specific messages favoring gender equity. There are some people who may object to this message. Their objections may be based on their political viewpoints and leanings. They may seek to have the policy changed, they may organize a campaign to elect new board members with different views, and they can do other things—but they do not have a *constitutional* right to demand that the board adopt a contrary policy.

"Opponents of the board's gender equity policy do not, for example, have a constitutional right to demand that the school adopt a policy favoring boys' sports over girls' sports. Or take another example, your honor." Sorowski was moving with confidence. He had prepared and he knew his material.

"The U-32 website currently includes an announcement about an African Library Project, seeking to raise funds to build a library in Malawi. This announcement, I would submit, is an illustration of speech by the school as an institution, whether or not it was students who may have promoted and even brought this project to fruition. Imagine a hypothetical student group opposed to spending funds on Malawi—let's call it *Students for America First*. They might demonstrate, might write letters, and so on, but they would not have the *constitutional right* to demand space on the school website to disseminate their own message.

"The school's website is *not* a public forum; it is reserved for school-sponsored speech. The school board gets to choose which messages it wants to sponsor and convey. And this principle applies—I think I'm getting to the heart of your question now, Judge Wallis—even when the message might be characterized as disseminating the school's viewpoint on a matter of political controversy."

"Civics," said the judge.

"I beg your pardon?"

"Civics," she repeated. "A public school can teach civics. Isn't that what you're talking about? The school can choose a curriculum that promotes a certain vision of democracy and liberty and equality. The school can teach *values*, yes?"

"Precisely so. The school can teach values. And the school can elect to use its flagpole to display symbols of its values. And at the same time, the school is required by the First Amendment to allow its students to express their views even if they are contrary to those values, so long as they do so in a manner that does not substantially disrupt the school's programs or interfere with the rights of other students."

Tad waited a moment to see if the judge had further questions. He nodded and sat down.

Croome stood immediately as the judge peered at him over her glasses. "Your honor," he said, "Board policies and websites and civics classes are irrelevant here. The Black Lives Matter flag was raised by and at the initiative of students of a certain political persuasion. My clients are students of a different political persuasion. They are being discriminated against."

"I've heard it," said Judge Wallis.

"Your honor?"

"I've heard your argument. I get it. You don't need to repeat it. Ms. Santana, I would like to assume your client does not have a pressing need to make additional arguments?"

Alicia took the cue. "No, not a pressing need, your honor."

"Very well," said the judge, her arthritis evidently causing her pain. "I hope to issue a written decision on the motion soon."

She nodded at the court officer, who bellowed, "All rise!"

The judge left the bench and disappeared through a side door. The lawyers shook hands as is common practice in Vermont courtrooms. Gerald Croome introduced his associate attorney and the paralegal who had been sharing the plaintiff's table. Tad, who held an adjunct faculty position at Vermont Law School, where he taught a course on municipal law, knew the associate as a former student in the class, and they spent a moment reminiscing.

Meanwhile, the paralegal, a solidly built young man in a good suit, approached Alicia and told her he would have liked to hear her argument. She didn't quite hear his name and before she could answer, the court officer, who seemed to have inherited the judge's impatience and her pained movements, interrupted: "Time to clear out and lock up," he said, and ushered them all out of the courtroom.

Alicia returned to her office after the hearing. "How you doing, Sam?" she said to her long-time law partner as she encountered him in the hallway with his coat on. He was heading out the door.

"Just fine, Alicia." Sam put his hand on her arm and asked, "Would you join me at Sacred Grounds for a coffee? Do you have a few minutes?"

Alicia nodded, smiling.

"I want to hear how the hearing went," Sam continued. "I was just on my way across the street." His usual afternoon break, the usual coffeehouse. Sam's practice was slowing down, easing up. Alicia had noticed he was losing some of his fire and some of his memory. How long ago did that start?

They crossed Chamber Street to the café. It was freezing outside. Inside, it was blissfully warm. A table was free, and Sam sat down. Alicia stood at the counter to order espresso for Sam, hot chai for herself, and then sat across from Sam.

"Judge Wallis," she told him, leaning forward, "was interested in both lines of precedent. By the way, I said nothing. But your worthy opponent, Tadeusz Sorowski, was brilliant."

Sorowski and Sam had been on opposite sides in the case challenging Ricky Stillwell's expulsion from high school, litigated before the same federal judge years earlier.

The barista at the counter yelled out, "Espresso! Chai!" Alicia brought the drinks to the table.

"What 'both lines of precedent'?" Sam asked. Alicia reminded him of *Summum* and *Hazelwood*. "Oh yes. I recall now," said Sam.

Acquaintances came by, exchanged greetings, and moved on. "How's Barb these days?" asked Sam, referring to Alicia's wife, who worked in the office at the Montpelier High School.

"Barb is fine. Never altogether at peace with life, you know, but fine. That's her nature. I always think she worries too much, and maybe that's getting worse. It's probably the times we're in." She tried the chai, still too hot. She blew on it. "But her work is going well. Better, for sure, than during the realm of Gayle Peters."

Sam chuckled at the memory. "Oy," was all he said.

Seven years earlier, the school's principal, Gayle Peters, had been fired after a scandal—one that emerged, in fact, from the testimony in Ricky's lawsuit. Alicia had represented the principal and helped her negotiate a decent settlement, but that was before the full extent of the scandal came to light—a tumultuous sexual relationship with a student—and the principal was sent off to prison.

Peters had been replaced by an interim principal, physics teacher John Carruthers, who served for a year. The board then hired a successor, who managed very well and stayed for five years. He was followed this year by long-time English teacher, Anna Duplessis, who decided to try her hand and turn her mind and skills toward administration. By all accounts, she was succeeding.

"You can imagine Barb's had to deal with a lot of change, Sam. She likes stability and she's not so keen on disruption. I think she's like you that way!" Alicia smiled warmly at her old friend. "But I can tell you, she's really pleased to be working for the latest new principal."

"I'm glad it's working out. The days of Gayle Peters seem long ago," he said.

The two nurtured their drinks quietly for a minute, while the coffeehouse buzzed around them. Reggae played through a speaker.

Sam asked, "So, how do you think our crafty, cranky judge will rule in your case?"

"Wallis? I think," answered Alicia with typical optimism, "the crafty, cranky judge will follow *Hazelwood* and *Summum* and dismiss the suit. Isn't it pretty clear?"

"No, it is not pretty clear," he instructed his junior partner. "The law is not clear."

"You old curmudgeon," she said. "With respect, of course."

It was the hour when school got out, and some high school students came into the café. Alicia recognized two of them from the Montpelier High School Racial Justice Alliance, whom Alicia had met at an Alliance meeting a month earlier at Sarah's invitation, where she'd been asked to talk about the Second Amendment lawsuit.

The students came over to Alicia and Sam's table to say hello. One, she remembered, was Manny Cruz, a beautiful boy, shy and vulnerable. The other, the girl, was beautiful too, with broad hips and magnificent curves. She carried herself with confidence, easily smiling at Alicia, while Manny avoided her eyes and looked around the place.

The girl said, "I know you're the lawyer and I remember your name. Alicia. From the Alliance meeting? I'm Kaliya Henderson. We met."

"I remember," said Alicia, smiling broadly. "How've you been?"

"Cool," she said. "What's happening in the lawsuit these days?"

There was a third chair at their table, and Alicia pointed to a free chair at the table next to them. "Bring it over. Sit," she said.

Manny brought over the chair and he and Kaliya took off their jackets and hung them on the backs of their chairs.

Alicia said, "This is my law partner, Sam Jacobson. Sam, Kaliya and Manny." She started to explain about the court hearing that day. She stopped to ask, "You want something to eat or drink?"

Sam cast a skeptical look at Alicia, like he was questioning her judgment. Maybe he doesn't want the company, she thought. He could be impatient. Too bad.

"Nah, I'm good," said Kaliya.

"Maybe I'll get something," said Manny. "Like a cookie? You sure, Kaliya?"

Kaliya changed her mind, and they went to the counter to order.

"Come on, Sam, stay for this," said Alicia.

"Why?"

"Because it's great to talk to these kids, and you've got nothing better on your plate."

"Probably right," said Sam. "You're having a good time."

The coffeeshop was humming. Bob Marley was urging them to get up and stand up for their rights.

Manny and Kaliya returned to the table. Manny had a peanut butter cookie. Kaliya said, "I got a mocha drink coming."

Alicia talked about the legal case and gave an outline of the arguments in court.

"What if they win?" asked Manny. "What happens then?"

Alicia leaned forward and touched Manny's hand. "Not really sure," she said. "The school could be ordered to raise the Second Amendment flag on the pole, but I doubt that would happen. The school could be ordered to remove the BLM flag and issue a policy that only official state and national flags can go up the flagpole. They'd probably have to pay some money to the plaintiffs and cover their attorneys' fees. But, first, you know, the school district would have to consider whether to appeal."

"Where would the appeal go?"

"That's to a court called the Second Circuit Court of Appeals. It sits in New York."

"You been there before?" asked Manny.

Alicia nodded.

"Cool," said Manny.

"Tell her about the email," said Kaliya.

"What email is that?" asked Alicia.

Manny fiddled with his phone and handed it to Alicia. She read:

You spic Manny. You make me sick. Go home to Mexico.

Patriots rise!

Alicia murmured, "Oh, no, Manny." She gave the phone to Sam and asked the teens, "Do you know anything else about this, where it came from?"

Kaliya spoke up. "Thing is, I know this kid. He's in tenth grade and I seen him in my homeroom. There're three other tenth grade boys in the homeroom. I overheard them talking."

"I showed Kaliya my email," said Manny.

"This tenth grade kid—" began Kaliya again.

"Who, what's his name?" Alicia asked her.

"Um, I think it's Doug. Doug Frazier."

Alicia took notes on a napkin. "Like, with a Z?"

"I think so."

"Go on, Kaliya. What were they talking about?"

"Doug tells his friends, you know, the other kids, about his big brother—his name's Marty."

"Marty Frazier?" Alicia interrupted.

"Yeah. He's been out of school for a few years. I think he's a stepbrother? Marty works like as an excavator up at Page Brothers in Barre. I paid attention, because I sort of know Marty too."

"Marty's harassed Kaliya," said Manny.

"Harassed?"

"Yeah, he's called me racial names, you know. Like *Brown Sugar*. Not really mean. It's more like he flirts with me but using racial code words. It's creepy."

"That's awful. I want to hear more about that, but can you go back to the other thing? His younger brother says something about him at school," prompted Alicia.

"Yeah, Doug says something to his friends about Marty being in a kind of gang called *The Patriots*. They do target practice and stuff."

Manny added, "See, when I showed that email to Kaliya, she thought it might have something to do with Marty, because of the word *Patriots*."

Kaliya added, "Marty's not talking about the football team."

"For sure not," Alicia nodded gravely.

"And you know what else?" said Kaliya.

"What else?"

"I seen Doug Frazier hanging out with Collin Chapman too, that kid who goes to U-32. They're buddies."

"Collin Chapman, the plaintiff in the lawsuit?"

"Yeah, that one."

Montpelier police detective Barry LaPorte was sitting in an FBI office in Burlington, up on the sixth floor of the Fred I. Parker Federal Courthouse building, with Special Agent Ed Duffy. They had a view of Lake Champlain, gray as slate. Duffy was small and compressed, a young mid-thirties, white, light hair trimmed close to his head, wearing a suit, neat as a pin. LaPorte was also a white man but appeared to be different in almost every other way: sixties and large and disheveled and rumpled, like an unmade bed.

Duffy was known for his research on white supremacy and militia groups around the country. "This group, The Patriots," said Duffy, pronouncing it *pie-triots* in a southern twang, "they're small in this part of Vermont. They're really just a group of guys with guns based in East Barre. They're not on the Web much themselves. But see this?"

Duffy was at the computer and pulled up a website for a militia group located south of Rutland on the other end of the state. "This group in Pawlet is much more organized. They own a large tract of land and conduct para-military trainings."

"I guess I've heard of them."

"Those guys," continued Duffy, "are pretty open about what they do. They post publicly on their own Facebook page—photos of bunkers with machine guns and boxes of ammunition. They allude to politicians who they say should be *taken out*. They're also always getting into trouble with their neighbors and town officials. I mean they're terrifying their neighbors. You can hear machine gun fire and even explosions on their property.

"And the town is upset, too, because they're in violation of local zoning laws. These neighbors who are complaining, so you know, they're not hippies and peaceniks; they're gun owners and hunters themselves. Here, look at this, Barry," Duffy said, pulling up an image on one of the group's posts: a closeup of a rifle and scope held by a person wearing a balaclava; above the photo were the words *THE ENEMY IS URBAN AND IT'S GETTING CLOSER*.

"Fucked up," said Barry.

"Now, I looked into this other thing for you," Duffy went on, as he scrolled through the website for Second Amendment, Inc. "Second Amendment's kind of a front group for a host of other groups. They have a Virginia office and they're the ones who raise the money. They talk a nicer game than the Pawlet folks. But see the links on this page—Patriots California, Patriots Arizona, and these other ones.

"Those groups are much larger and more organized, of course, than the outfit in East Barre. They do a lot of private border patrolling, stuff like that. Here's what I want you to know: They all get money from Second Amendment, Inc."

"How do you know that?"

"I checked the revenue sources on the 990s filed by the larger Patriots groups, their tax returns. They're available to the public. All of them list Second Amendment as a major source, if not *the* major source."

LaPorte asked, "Is the Vermont group affiliated with them?"

"We don't see connections with the militia outfit in Pawlet. They may not be part of the same network. But, interestingly, we think the East Barre fellows might be. We haven't connected all the links yet. The East Barre group doesn't file a 990, so we can't connect them that way."

"And Marty Frazier? Is he in your database there?"

"Oh yes. He's got some history with the state police—domestic assault, more than once, leading to illegal weapons charges. When he's in the system, he starts talking far right extremist ideology, so the state police let us know about him. But we didn't know he was connected to The Patriots. Not until now."

Putting the bits and pieces of information together into an affidavit, Detective LaPorte procured a search warrant authorizing the police to seize and search electronic communications devices from Martin Frazier. In the early morning, LaPorte showed up at the Page Brothers yard in Barre Town, where four or five guys were standing, some with plastic coffee cups in hand, next to the trucks and bucket loaders. They watched him emerge from the squad car.

"Hoy," began LaPorte, "morning to you." Friendly enough but not jovial.

"Morning, officer," said one.

"Is one of you Martin Frazier?" he asked.

"That's me," said a bearded man wearing a brown denim jacket streaked with dried mud. His expression was surly, much as LaPorte had expected.

"Can I talk to you over here by my car?"

Marty walked over to the car.

"You got a smartphone, Mr. Frazier?"

"Why's that?" asked Mr. Frazier.

"Fair question," said LaPorte. "As it happens, I have a search warrant authorizing me to seize it, if you've got it." He showed Frazier the warrant.

"What the fuck. What for?"

"Well, that's a good question too, but I'm not here to discuss that. I'm here to take the phone."

Frazier looked around to see if his buddies could help. They watched without moving. He glanced over at a pick-up truck parked nearby. LaPorte figured the truck belonged to Frazier, and Frazier was spinning ideas about making a run for it.

"Now, Mr. Frazier, what I'm going to tell you to do is this: You reach carefully into your back pocket, where I can see your phone is, and you hand it to me now."

Frazier said, "I done nothing wrong," and kept looking around. He appeared confused about this sudden turn in the direction of his life.

LaPorte, the larger man, took one step toward Frazier. Frazier pulled the phone from his pocket and held it up. "You want this? No fucking way."

LaPorte anticipated Frazier's movements and grabbed his arm before he could throw the phone into the brush next to LaPorte's cruiser, as if that would have done much good. LaPorte wrenched it out of Frazier's hand.

Frazier yelled, "You fucking assaulted me! You can't do this. I got rights."

"Thank you, sir," said the detective. "Yes, you do have rights. Let me ask you this, you got a computer, a laptop, anything like that at home?"

"What?"

"If you lie to me, that's a criminal offense. You have a computer or laptop or tablet at home?"

"I got a laptop."

"Can you see if you can get a half hour off from work and we'll drive together to your house and I'll be taking the laptop too."

"No fucking way," he said.

"All right then," said the detective. "I can go myself. I know where you live. The warrant authorizes me to do that. I might need to break the lock."

Frazier stared at him. Then he said, "I'll drive my truck." He did so, with LaPorte close behind in the cruiser.

Later the same day, an IT guy who worked for the FBI examined Frazier's phone and laptop. He found that Frazier himself had sent the threatening emails to Sarah and Manny. Not only that, he also located communications between Marty Frazier and someone called Neil Davison at Second Amendment, Inc., with Frazier reporting on his activities and Davison referencing payments to be made to Frazier. An email from Davison said, "Keep at it. Make them bleed."

A subsequent warrant application gave the police access to Frazier's bank records. Money had been wired during the last two months to Frazier from an account owned by Second Amendment, Inc. Three payments of $1,000 each.

In the interviews with LaPorte and his FBI counterparts, Marty Frazier was both truculent and ultimately cooperative. He told them he had sent the letters to Sarah and Sorowski too. He wanted a deal. He gave up names and connections and details. The locals were in bed with Second Amendment, Inc.

Neither the Feds nor the Vermont Attorney General decided to charge Martin Frazier. They were interested in the bigger picture. They told Frazier sternly to behave himself and to stick around for further questioning if warranted.

Part III

Damages

When Sarah hears the man outside her darkened cell again, she speaks up. "Why are you doing this?"

"What do you mean?" he asks, appearing a few seconds later with his mask at the little window in the downstairs bathroom door.

"Why are you holding me here like this?"

"I told you we want to stop your damn lawsuit."

"But why is that so important to you? To you personally." She didn't really know where she was going with this. She needed to talk.

"You don't get it, do you? Listen. We're turning into a minority here, and in the rest of the country. Vermont used to be white. Black people are coming across into Vermont from New York State or Massachusetts and wherever. You turn on the TV? You see black people all the time.

"We got Mexicans and whatnot swamping across the border in fucking caravans down there. Excuse my French. They're gang members and rapists. I don't recognize my country. We're being *replaced*. Don't you care about that? Maybe you don't, cuz you're Jewish—*Jacobson*. Jesus."

Sarah looks at the Trump mask, unsure how to respond. She is weary and defeated but has enough sense to try not to exacerbate the man's anger. She finally says, without much conviction, "We're all just people, trying our best to live our lives."

"You are Jewish though."

She thinks on it. "I'm not religious at all," she tells him. "I'm not observant."

"I'm not *observant* either, but I'm still a Christian. And you're a Jew."

"Okay, but so what?"

"Jews always try to run things. They hold the power. Remember Madeleine Kunin? She was governor. You know she was Jewish? No kidding! My parents both grew up in Vermont, right here in Thetford." He stops. "Oh shit! I weren't supposed to tell you that. Don't say nothing about that."

She waits a beat. "I won't say anything, Jack."

"Good, you better not. So yeah, we Vermonters go back. My grandparents too. My dad says it never were like it is now. We took care of ourselves. We took care of the land, you know? We didn't need Montpelier and all its lawyers and laws and shit."

Sarah said, "I understand things have changed." She saw the mask at the little window, but she couldn't tell whether he was looking at her. She realized, strangely, she wanted to see his face.

"Oh yeah, they *changed*." His voice was bitter. "Like when my dad was a kid, we didn't have racial people here or Jews or, you know, Arab-type people. Fucking Muslims now. Okay, so I already let it outta the bag we're in Thetford. You know what? We're next to the old town poor farm. The people here used to take care of our own poor. They farmed right here on this road, lived right here. You don't need Montpelier to run everything. Way too much government now where it don't belong. You know what happened with my dad?"

"I don't," said Sarah. "What happened to your dad?"

"He run a gas station in the village, the other side of Tucker Hill. My grandfather had it before that. Guess what? Montpelier told him he needed to replace the tanks and the gas pumps. Then they denied his fucking permit cuz the pumps was too close to the road or too close to the neighbors or something. My family'd been selling gas for over forty years. Goddamn bureaucrats wanting to run everyone's lives. Fucking ruin their lives, more like it. They ruined him. He's got nothing now. Swears at the TV all day."

"I'm not trying to run everything," she says uselessly. She is exhausted and hungry. She thinks she might have made a fatal mistake asking him this question. She can barely stand.

"Yeah, you are. You're trying to take people's guns and shut down Second Amendment and that's not right, just because Marty Frazier sent you a bunch of crazy emails or whatever." The man ducks down and Sarah hears him swearing and groaning. "Shit again, I didn't mean to say names like that." He waits.

"I won't tell about that either," Sarah says. She already knows about Marty Frazier.

"Marty didn't mean anything by it anyways. He just does crazy stuff like that."

It dawns on Sarah that she is putting herself in more jeopardy every time the man reveals something else about himself or where they are. To her horror she suddenly understands he can't release her if she has the information to find him.

She draws her breath in sharply and audibly.

"You okay there, Sarah?" asks the man through his mask, his voice much softer at the edges. "Look, you may be Jewish, but I think you're fine, like a fine person."

She swallows. "Thank you for saying that, Jack." She waits to see what he does next. "I'm a little hungry again," she tells him. "Would you be able to bring me something, maybe fruit if you have any?"

"Yeah, I'll look and see what I got upstairs. But, you know, we have a right to have guns, to protect our families, our way of life. You got to understand that. Who knows what's coming? Fucking Feds could be at your doorstep anytime."

Judge Wallis issued the federal court's ruling on a Thursday in March of 2019. The judge relied upon *Summum* and *Walker* to dismiss Second Amendment's lawsuit. The flagpole, she wrote, is not a forum for students to engage in expression. It is school property, and it is the school's province to decide to fly the BLM flag and not to fly another group's flag.

For good measure, the judge found that there could be no genuine dispute that the school administration's support of BLM related to legitimate pedagogical concerns, namely, the desire to foster a more inclusive, diverse, and equitable school environment that welcomed racial minorities, even if the methods the school chose led to divisive controversy.

Should Second Amendment wish to appeal from the order dismissing its complaint, it had thirty days to decide.

Later on that same Thursday afternoon, Alicia and Sam invited Sarah and Tad and Sherise Bailey, the school superintendent, to their office, where the five of them toasted Judge Wallis and the Black Lives Matter movement, and four of them drank champagne. Sherise did not drink and could stay for only a minute as she was in a rush to prepare for a special meeting of the school board.

"Damn, this feels good," Sherise said, standing up to excuse herself. "For the moment, right?"

Sam engaged. "Why just the moment?"

Sherise, at the doorway, turned to look back at Sam. "I don't think it's over. Chickens'll come home to roost and all that. I've got an entire school district to think about—six different schools, with all kinds of unpredictable behavior. How am I supposed to keep it all sane? I'm not sleeping well, you know? Lord help me."

"You take care, Sherise," said Alicia. "I hear you."

"Blessings," said Sherise, and they watched her go.

Alicia poured herself another glass of champagne. "Anyone else?" she asked. Sam held out his glass and Alicia filled it. Tad declined. Sarah took the bottle from Alicia and poured for herself. They sat for a while in silence, a savored victory, tempered by the superintendent's premonition.

"Sarah and I have been talking, Tad," said Alicia, after a suitable interval, waving the glass in her hand, "about bringing a case under Vermont's civil hate-crime law."

"Yes?"

"What we want to do is go after the national organization for instigating hate crimes and threats here in Vermont."

"You mean sue Second Amendment?"

"Right. Exactly. The plaintiffs would be you, Sarah, and Manny Cruz, everyone who got a threatening letter or email."

"Can we prove the national group is responsible for the hate mail?"

"I think we can. In fact, Marty Frazier can be our witness on that. He already made statements to the FBI that they paid him a bunch of money based on what he was doing to stop the BLM movement here. Marty's nasty but he'll be our witness."

"He won't cooperate."

"Fine, we'll subpoena him, and we can hold him to his sworn statement to the FBI. The Richmond Virginia folks knew what he was doing and were *paying* him to do it."

"What about damages, Alicia?" Tad skeptically continued. "We don't have substantial damages, I think."

"I think we do, but even so, Tad, look at the statute. 13 V.S.A. § 1457 authorizes not just compensatory damages but also punitive damages and attorney's fees.[1] What I'm thinking is, we ask a Vermont jury to go out and grant us a huge punitive damages award against them. Enough to shut them down. That's what motivates me."

"Ah hah. Let me see the statutes. Do you have Title 13?"

"Do I have Title 13," she mocked. Alicia brought him the volume from her office, with post-it notes stuck on the applicable pages.

"All right," he said. "I see how section 1457 authorizes broad remedies, including punitive damages, in a civil action. We must, however, prove the plaintiffs suffered injury as a result of conduct prohibited by section 1455. Now, 1455 is the actual hate-crime

---

1   13 V.S.A. § 1457 provides: "Independent of any criminal prosecution or the result thereof, any person suffering damage, loss, or injury as a result of conduct prohibited by section 1455 . . . of this title may bring an action for injunctive relief, compensatory and punitive damages, costs and reasonable attorney's fees, and other appropriate relief against any person who engaged in such conduct."

enhancement statute.[2] A person who commits a crime, and it's motivated—maliciously motivated—by the victim's race, color, and so forth, is subject to additional punishment. All right, but there must still be an underlying crime. 1455 enhances the penalties of the underlying crime when it is motivated by racial bias. What would you say is the underlying crime here?"

"Extortion is one, threatening is another, stalking is a third, disorderly conduct is a fourth," Alicia said. "Here, let me have the book. Okay. Take a look at 13 V.S.A. § 1701, the law making extortion a crime. It says:

> *A person who maliciously threatens to accuse another of a crime or offense, or with an injury to his or her person or property, with intent to extort money or other pecuniary advantage, or with intent to compel the person so threatened to do an act against his or her will, shall be imprisoned not more than three years or fined not more than $500.00, or both.*

"It's not quite grammatical, I know, but that describes the conduct."

"You would argue that Second Amendment engaged in extortion, Alicia?"

"They weren't trying to extort money, but they were threatening to injure you guys with the intent to compel you to do an act against your will. That's extortion too. More precisely, they were using Marty Frazier as their agent to accomplish that purpose."

"An act against our will?" Tad continued to press for a complete understanding.

"Right. They were trying to get you to drop the BLM campaign, against your will. They were trying to damage the campaign. Why else?"

2   13 V.S.A. § 1455 provides: "A person who commits, causes to be committed, or attempts to commit any crime and whose conduct is maliciously motivated by the victim's actual or perceived race, color, religion, national origin, sex, ancestry, age, service in the U.S. Armed Forces, disability . . ., sexual orientation, or gender identity shall be subject to the following penalties: . . . ."

"I wasn't personally involved in the BLM campaign," said Tad.

"Come on, Tad. You're the lawyer representing the school district that's flying the flag. These guys are threatening you to try to make you afraid of defending the school's decisions. Give me a break here."

"Yes, I see your point, Alicia."

"And now check out criminal threatening in 13 V.S.A. § 1702. That doesn't require extortion, just a threat. Here. It says a person shall not by words or conduct knowingly threaten another person, and as a result of the threat, place the other person in reasonable apprehension of death or serious bodily injury."

"That is a high standard, Alicia. Death or serious bodily injury."

"*Reasonable* apprehension of death or serious bodily injury. Did Frazier put you and the others in that state of fear? And keep in mind, Tad, we'd be pursuing a *civil* action. We don't need to prove the facts beyond a reasonable doubt, even though the conduct is set forth in the criminal code. Preponderance of the evidence; that's our standard."

"Meaning what?" asked Sarah.

"Meaning our burden of proof is not as high as the burden of proof in a criminal case. Right? To get a conviction in a criminal case, the prosecution needs to demonstrate guilt beyond a reasonable doubt. That's really tough to do. But to prevail in a civil suit, the plaintiff needs only to demonstrate that the defendant caused harm to the plaintiff by what's called the preponderance of the evidence. Which means showing that's the more likely way things happened."

"Regardless," said Tad, "I am not certain I can say that I was in reasonable apprehension of death or serious injury when I got that letter."

Sarah spoke again. "I was. Ricky sure thinks I was."

"I think she was too," Sam finally spoke. "And is. And so are you, Tad, if you listen to your true feelings."

"My true feelings are horror that this sort of behavior is going on in our world. I am less concerned for my own safety."

"Yes, I can appreciate that," Sam conceded.

"Now, check out the stalking statutes." Alicia was eager to continue her exposition of the basis for a lawsuit. "The term *stalk* is defined in 13 V.S.A. § 1061(4), here."

Tad took the volume and read the section out loud:

> *"Stalk" means to engage purposefully in a course of conduct directed at a specific person that the person engaging in the conduct knows or should know would cause a reasonable person to fear for his or her safety or the safety of another or would cause a reasonable person substantial emotional distress.*

"Emotional distress," said Alicia. "Your horror. That we can prove for certain. And the operative section is 1062," she said as she took the book back. "'Any person who intentionally stalks another person shall be imprisoned not more than two years or fined not more than $5,000.00, or both.'

"Second Amendment, acting through its agent Marty Frazier, was stalking you. They were purposefully engaged in conduct directed at specific individuals, knowing they were threatening your safety and knowing their actions would cause you emotional distress. *Make them bleed*, their man said. The organization can be held *civilly* liable, and made to pay punitive damages, for committing these sorts of crimes."

"Who said, *Make them bleed*?" asked Sam.

"It was the guy in the Second Amendment central office in Virginia, giving *instruction* to Marty Frazier."

"Okay, right. And can a person commit a stalking offense through the mail or by email?"

"Yes. That's one way it's done. Probably the most common way these days. Stay with me."

"I'm trying, Alicia!" said Sam.

"There are at least two more underlying offense statutes. Disorderly conduct is one. 13 V.S.A. § 1026(a) states that a person is guilty of disorderly conduct if they have an intent to cause public inconvenience or annoyance and they then engage in *threatening* behavior. It's another way the law criminalizes certain threatening behavior. And the second is disturbing the peace by use of electronic communications. 13 V.S.A. § 1027(a)."

"Slow down, Alicia, please." Tad was ever cautious. "You said the premise of a disorderly conduct violation is the intent to cause *public* inconvenience or annoyance. Can we establish the intent element?"

Alicia beamed at Tad. "Ah. You're noticing that word *public*. And that's a point I hadn't focused on. I can do a little more research on that piece."

"All right. The second statute you just mentioned, electronic . . . ?"

"Communications. I'll read it:

> *A person who, with intent to terrify, intimidate, threaten, harass, or annoy makes contact by means of a telephonic or other electronic communication with another and . . . threatens to inflict injury or physical harm to the person or property of any person . . . shall be fined not more than $250.00 or be imprisoned not more than three months, or both.*

"Frazier had the intent to intimidate and threaten. That's element number one. He used electronic communications for at least some of his messages. That's two. And three, he did threaten to inflict injury. I think we can prove that too."

They sat in silence for a few moments.

Tad spoke. "I wonder, Alicia, whether we might incur a risk by pursuing this course of action."

"What risk—of losing the lawsuit, or having attorney's fees imposed on us?"

"No, not that. I feel, I am afraid to say, much as Sherise Bailey indicated she feels. I worry about how irrational and perhaps how violent some of these True Patriot people might be. I'm listening to my true feelings, you see, Sam?

"After all, Alicia, your premise is that they are truly threatening harm. We know they use guns. Bringing a lawsuit to extinguish the organization might just pull the trigger," Tad smiled weakly, "to use an unfortunate metaphor. They may elect to exercise their Second Amendment rights, as some people might say."

Sarah said, "I can't imagine that would really happen."

"I don't know," said Sam, who was at the sink washing the glasses. "I agree with Tad. There could be a risk with this. But I also think there may be legal problems with the case. Remember the Westboro Baptist Church?"

Her father was always the pessimist, thought Sarah. "I remember the Church," she said. "They were homophobic to the extreme. I'm not sure what happened to them."

"There was a Supreme Court decision, maybe ten years ago. Let me find it." He went to the wall of legal books and started thumbing through Supreme Court Reporter volumes from the approximate era.

Meanwhile, Sarah got out her phone and googled *Westboro Baptist*, announcing, "It's a 2011 decision, called *Snyder v. Phelps.*"

Sam found the case. "Okay, Roberts wrote the majority opinion. The case involves church members picketing near a soldier's funeral service. The father of the soldier whose funeral it was brought suit for money damages against members of the Westboro Baptist Church. The claim was intentional infliction of emotional distress.

"That's a type of tort claim, Sarah, under the state's common law. The jury in the trial court found in favor of the father and awarded huge damages. When the appeal percolates up to the Supreme Court, the question presented," Sam read from the opinion, "is whether the First Amendment shields the church members' picketing from tort liability. And the Supreme Court's answer is yes, the picketing is protected First Amendment speech."

"Hold on for a second," Sarah said. She was puzzled. "How does the First Amendment come into it? It's not the government censoring their speech, right? It's a suit brought by the soldier's family."

"That is an astute question, Sarah." A rare compliment from the father. "And I think the answer goes like this: if the state law, even common law torts, as in this case, provides a right of action in court, allowing private citizens to restrain the speech—and a judge can punish or even enjoin the speech of the protestors as a result—then the *state* is involved in restraining the speech of the protestors and that is why the First Amendment is triggered. Did I get that right, Alicia?"

"That's it, Sam." Alicia beamed her gorgeous smile, pleased that Sam had asked her for confirmation.

Sam continued to consult the Supreme Court opinion. "Their picket signs, by the way, were truly awful, with messages like *Thank God for Dead Soldiers* and *You're Going to Hell*. The court talked about the principle that debate on public issues should be uninhibited, robust, and wide-open, quoting *New York Times v. Sullivan*. Then it found that the content of the Westboro signs was related to broad issues of interest to society at large—matters of public import—no matter how hideous."

"This doesn't bother me," said Alicia. "As a legal matter, I mean. As awful as it is, the Westboro people were still engaged in a public protest, right?"

"Fair enough," said Sam. "But targeted at a particularly vulnerable family, who brought suit under state law to recover for their emotional injuries. Like you would be doing, in effect."

"Does this mean our case would be dismissed under the First Amendment?"

"No, Sarah, I don't think it does," Alicia argued. "I think there must be a difference when a person is not protesting in a public place but sending targeted threatening letters to individuals." She held up a finger while she paused.

"No, sorry, I think I've got that wrong. It doesn't matter if the speech act happens in a public place. What makes the difference—this is it—is whether the speech is truly a *threat*. Right? What was the cross-burning case? *Virginia v. Black*, maybe?"

She turned to Sarah. Sarah again consulted the world through her phone. "*Virginia v. Black*, 123 S. Ct. 1536. Decided in 2003."

Alicia pulled the volume off the shelf. "This involved," she said after a moment of reading, "review of convictions for violating a State of Virginia statute that criminalized burning a cross on another person's property or on public property, with the intent of intimidating a person or a group. This was an O'Connor opinion.

"The court held that a state *may* ban cross burning when it is done with the intent to intimidate someone. True threats are not considered protected speech under the First Amendment. Okay?" She read from the text. "Here's what the court says about that:

> *True threats encompass those statements where the speaker means to communicate a serious expression of an intent to commit an act of unlawful violence to a particular individual or group of individuals. The speaker need not actually intend to carry out the threat. Rather, a prohibition on true threats protects individuals from the fear of violence and from the disruption that fear engenders, in addition to protecting people from the possibility that the threatened violence will occur.*

"I'm skipping the citations. See, in the *Westboro* case, the church people didn't communicate an intent to commit violence against the soldier's family."

"Something very close to that, it seems to me," Sarah pushed.

"I suppose you're right, Sarah," said Alicia. "But I do appreciate that a sign at a funeral that says *You'll burn in Hell* does not communicate the same level of intent to hurt someone, at least in the here and now, as burning a cross on a person's yard in certain communities and contexts. The exceptions to the broad protection the First Amendment affords to controversial speech are *narrow*. As they should be, because we want the freedom of speech itself to be broad. Without that principle, *we* lose the right to protest the government."

Alicia looked up to see if the group was following. At the moment, they were, and she was facing no argument from Sam or Tad. She said, "Let me read another passage from the *Virginia* case:

> *The First Amendment permits Virginia to outlaw cross burnings done with the intent to intimidate because burning a cross is a particularly virulent form of intimidation. Instead of prohibiting all intimidating messages, Virginia may choose to regulate this subset of intimidating messages in light of cross burning's long and pernicious history as a signal of impending violence.*

"So that's the question, right?" Alicia snapped the book shut. "The cases can be reconciled. Westboro's actions were horrible, for sure, but they did not amount to a serious threat of violence against the intended recipients. So, Westboro's protest was protected speech, and the soldier's family was barred from suing the church for damages.

"But when the KKK burns a cross with an intent to intimidate or, really, to give the message, the *serious expression*, that they *intend to commit* acts of violence against specific victims, that expression of violent intent is not protected speech under the First Amendment."

Tad stepped in with his customary formality. "Hence, according to your reasoning as I understand it, the law ought to permit vindication of a damages claim against Second Amendment, Inc., because it engaged in a sort of expressive conduct that constituted a true threat of violence aimed specifically at Green Mountain BLM and at particular individuals. That is to say, *us*."

Sam grumbled, "You're right. It's winnable."

Alicia addressed Tad. "Does this mean you're in? Can I represent you?"

"I am favorably inclined, Alicia."

"Me, being your lawyer—it just makes me blush, Tad."

At the next meeting of the Green Mountain Black Lives Matter board, held in the Montpelier High School library, Samantha Janey brought Alicia and Sarah in to explain the case. She asked Manny Cruz to come to the meeting too. He and his parents had already agreed to participate in the lawsuit.

Alicia began with an outline of the law and the proposed suit. The initial reaction was puzzlement.

"Read the letters," Sarah suggested to Alicia.

The board members' attitude shifted to outrage once they heard the language in the messages sent to Sarah, Tad, and Manny.

Chip Skinner, the board chair, queried whether their organization, GMBLM, might be included as one of the plaintiffs.

"Glad you asked," Alicia said. "The answer is yes. It makes sense because the threats are aimed at the work of the organization. Sarah and Manny are obviously targeted as effective BLM organizers seeking racial justice. Attorney Tad Sorowski is targeted because he represents U-32, the school defending their right to fly the BLM flag. It's an attack against the movement itself."

"They're also targeted based on their ethnicity and religion," said Elena, the student member from U-32 who had been at Sarah's job interview.

"That's the most insidious part," said Alicia, "and it's what makes this group, Second Amendment, liable under the hate crime statute—that they targeted individuals based on that sort of characteristic. That is the key to the courtroom."

"What risks do you see for the organization?" asked Samantha Janey, her arms crossed. "If we go forward."

"Not much risk," Alicia answered. "At least, I don't see significant financial risk. My firm would take the case on a contingency basis. Meaning we don't get paid any fees unless we win or settle. We, the firm, would want our out-of-pocket costs paid back regardless. Costs for depositions, things like that, which might amount to two or three thousand dollars or less, I'd guess, depending on how the litigation goes.

"But as for the legal fees, the firm would accept the risk. It's also important to know that the hate crimes statute, under which we would bring the suit, has a fee-shifting provision. What that means is that, if we prevail, Second Amendment would be ordered to pay back our fees."

"What if," asked Samantha, "we lose in court?"

"That's where my law firm takes the risk. In that case, we don't get paid for the work we do. The fee-shifting provision in the law, by the way, is not reciprocal. If we lose, you would not be required to pay the attorney's fees incurred by Second Amendment."

"What do you think the odds are?" This came from the board member and legislator from Norwich.

"What I can say is, I wouldn't take the case if I didn't think we had the stronger position. We have to prove a few things: that sending these messages to these individuals is the kind of threatening conduct prohibited by the Vermont statutes; that Second Amendment is responsible for getting this local guy, Marty Frazier, to do what he did; and that Sarah, Tad, and Manny felt the level of fear and distress that the statutes describe. In short, liability, causation, and injury.

"Beyond that, we have to be prepared to defeat what Second Amendment, Inc., will undoubtedly raise as its chief defense, that penalizing them for sending these messages is unconstitutional under the First Amendment. We've looked pretty closely at that argument. We have the stronger position."

Samantha spoke up again. "Alicia, you said before you didn't think we faced a financial risk. But you didn't really address whether you see other risks."

Alicia took a long moment over this one.

"I don't know," she finally said. "How will it go down politically? You can judge this better than I can. I think your allies will be in full support. Your opponents, of course, will not. But will it make things worse? Will your agenda become more difficult as a result of a suit like this? Frankly, I don't know. If we win, of course, I've got to think it will mobilize support and energize the movement."

Sarah joined in. "If we win big, with punitive damages, then we put a huge dent in the white supremacist movement. As Alicia said from the start, the goal of this lawsuit is to shut down Second Amendment, Inc."

"And maybe in the process of doing that," Alicia added, "we get to transfer some of their resources to Black Lives Matter."

"That could happen?" asked one of the students on the board.

"It could," Alicia replied. "It's a bit early to say how likely it is. That's the upside. I've got to say, though, there is another kind of downside risk in filing a suit like this that should be spoken out loud. The lawsuit could be seen as an invitation to bring it on, if you know what I mean. It might aggravate tensions. It might provoke a violent response."

The words hung in the air for a minute.

Samantha said, "We can't be afraid. This is our opportunity to make change."

No one disputed that in the silence that followed. Chip, the board chair, then suggested the board should temporarily excuse their guests—Alicia, Sarah, and Manny—so the board could discuss the matter on its own.

Fifteen minutes later, the guests were invited back from the hallway into the library room. Chip told them the board was prepared to join the suit as a plaintiff and had authorized him to review and sign a fee agreement with the Jacobson & Santana firm along the lines they had discussed. "We're in," he said, grinning at his colleagues.

Elena, the student board member who'd spoken to Sarah earlier, came up to her as the meeting wrapped up. "I had heard generally about those letters, Sarah. But I didn't know exactly what they said until tonight. It's really horrible."

"Sometimes I feel that," Sarah told her. "Other times I forget about them. Or ignore them. I think they upset me less than they should. They upset my partner, Ricky, more than me. I'm jaded, I guess."

"I think you might be in denial." The seventeen-year-old high school senior gazed at Sarah a moment, before saying, "Will you please take care, Sarah?"

Over the next week, Alicia drafted a complaint and went through a few rewrites with Sam. She circulated the draft to Sarah, Tad, and the Cruz family. With final edits, the complaint was ready for filing in state court.

Sarah and Samantha Janey worked on a press release. They wanted to make a public splash.

Second Amendment, Inc., retained the same Burlington law firm that had sued U-32 over the raising of the BLM flag. They defended the new lawsuit on a number of grounds.

Of course, one of the grounds was that Martin Frazier or his cohorts in the True Patriots group in East Barre, Vermont, did not act in this specific way at the behest of the national organization, and the latter could therefore not be held liable for the actions of the former. But they also argued that, even assuming the Patriots group acted as the agent of Second Amendment, the letter-writing campaign was protected speech under the First Amendment.

And for this reason, because they raised a critical defense arising under federal law, they shifted the case over to federal court. This is a privilege accorded to defendants—to "remove" a case from state court to federal court, when the defense relies on federal law.

Gerald Croome filed his answer and defenses and the removal petition in the last week of March 2019. He also filed his notice of appeal from Judge Wallis's order dismissing the earlier U-32 flag case. The appeal would move to the Second Circuit Court of Appeals in New York City.

Croome called Tad Sorowski soon after. "I'd like to meet with you to explore a settlement," he began. When Tad responded with surprise, Croome added, "Look, we've filed our appeal. We think we have a strong argument on appeal. But we're willing to withdraw the appeal as part of a settlement of both cases. I'd like to meet both with you and Alicia Santana to explore the idea of a global settlement."

The attorneys met on a gloomy, wet April day at Jacobson & Santana on Chamber Street to hear from Attorney Croome on his settlement proposal, whatever it would be. Croome appeared with his paralegal assistant, Keith Thomas. They hung their wet coats on the coat stand and joined Tad and Alicia around the firm's conference table, while a grumbling Sam made a pot of coffee in the old drip coffee maker.

"Sorry, we don't have milk or cream," he said.

Rain pattered on the windows of the conference room. After a few professional pleasantries, Croome got to the point. "We dismiss the appeal. You dismiss your lawsuit against Second Amendment. We all walk away, have a nice day, and save a lot of money."

The three other lawyers in the room shared skeptical glances.

"No, I do not think so, Mr. Croome." It was like Tad to use formalities.

"You won't consider my offer?"

The wind picked up outside, sending occasional blasts of rain drumming against the windows. Around the table Tad, Alicia, and Sam needed only slight headshakes to come to consensus.

Tad said, "I represent the school board in the flag case. I can have a discussion with you about settlement proposals relating to that case, and I can and will advise my client of any firm proposals you make regarding that case. I do not represent the plaintiffs in the hate crime suit. In fact, as you know, I am one of the plaintiffs."

"That is precisely why I requested this meeting with the three of you together," pursued Croome. He turned to address Sam. "I understand you're known to be something of a First Amendment lawyer, Sam. You have that reputation and I congratulate you. But in both of these cases, you are on the wrong side, defending violations of my client's civil liberties.

"That is true of my client's effort to fly its flag on the school flagpole once it was opened for use by the Black Lives Matter students. It is equally true of my client's desire to engage in political speech. Even if Second Amendment can be shown to be responsible for the emails and letters, it never issued a direct threat of imminent harm, as you contend. What we have is young people blowing off steam and using offensive language to express resentment at elites who interfere with their lives. You are seeking to censor speech that is protected under the First Amendment. I'm surprised."

Alicia was indignant that Croome addressed Sam and not her, the lawyer who wrote and signed the complaint against Second Amendment. Sexism was still pervasive in certain quarters of the Vermont bar. She was used to it, irritated by it, and sometimes confrontational about it. But at this moment, she held her tongue.

The lights suddenly went out in the building.

"You see," Alicia said to Gerald Croome, looking for humor in their common situation, "your attitude just caused a power outage."

In the dim natural light of the room, Sam would not be budged from his own irritation at Croome's patronizing insults. "It's an historical building. It happens. All I can say, Mr. Croome, is you're welcome to your opinion."

He noticed Croome's paralegal, Keith Thomas, watching him with a curious intensity. Thomas was dressed sharply in a pressed white shirt, a gray tie, and a tailored gray suit. Sam was wearing an old sweater with patched elbows. Sam now remembered Thomas from the federal court hearing with Judge Wallis the previous November.

"As you appear to be stubborn about the possibility of a global settlement," said Gerald Croome, swiveling his chair to address Tad again, "it might be useful to consider bifurcating our discussion. Perhaps we might discuss settling just the flag case at this moment."

He paused to see if there were a response. There was none, and Croome continued. "We have filed an appeal. Our withdrawing the appeal has value to you. How much value? Shall we say $40,000?"

Tad coughed. "I cannot imagine the school board would agree to pay that sum in view of the posture of the case at this time. We have prevailed in the district court."

"Nonetheless, you are at risk of losing it all on appeal. You know that. We have the resources, you understand, to pursue the appeal to the fullest extent. I am authorized by my clients to withdraw the appeal in exchange for payment of $40,000."

"You won't have any resources left if we're successful in our suit," grumbled Sam.

"I will respond to your proposal," said Tad, "after I have had the opportunity to consult with my client."

"Thank you, Tad, for your courtesy."

But Sam understood Croome's politeness to Tad as a backhanded insult directed to himself. "Now," said Croome, "may we explore whether the suit you have filed against Second Amendment, Inc., can be settled? My view, and I think I'm being objective here, is that these claims have almost no chance of success."

Croome was still directing his opinionated remarks to Sam, not to Alicia. Alicia made another chalk mark in her memory bank, and let it ride.

"You cannot tie the specific content of the letters," argued Croome, "to the national organization."

"Are you asking us if we will make a demand, or are you willing to put something on the table?" asked Sam.

"The latter. I am presently authorized," replied Croome, "to offer payment in the amount of $50,000 in exchange for full releases against Second Amendment, Inc., and any of its affiliated organizations, directors, officers, and so on."

"That's it?" said Sam.

"That's it. And I think it unlikely we will put more on the table. $50,000 is a large sum for us. We're a nonprofit."

Sam interrupted. "Yet you just said you had lots of resources."

"That is true as well. We can raise the money as needed to continue litigation, because of the loyal support we earn from members and donors. But the money is not in my client's bank account. I'm deliberately starting at a high number. You understand. It's a serious offer and I'm not playing games, Mr. Jacobson. We're not going to be nickel and dimed. That may be your style. It is not mine. I'm not going to get in the gutter with you."

Sam leaned back in his chair and stared at the lawyer. He noticed that Keith Thomas was looking at him again with that curious gaze, as if he were enjoying the joust. Sam glanced at Alicia, who put her hand over her brow as if soothing a headache. He looked at Tad, who gently shook his head back and forth with his jaw set firm.

"Mr. Croome," said Sam. "I am Jewish."

Croome immediately interrupted. "So? That's irrelevant."

"As I suspect you know. When you tell a Jew that his style is nickel-and-diming, and you are not getting into the gutter with him to squabble over money, as you say, that is the only relevant thing going on. Everything else fades to insignificance."

Croome crossed his arms over his chest. "It appears you are accusing me of anti-Semitism."

"I don't know what motivates you," Sam told him wearily. "But when you invoke vile anti-Semitic tropes, you are being offensive and counter-productive."

"Do you play that card often?" Croome asked derisively.

Sam stood, pushing his chair back. He wagged his index finger for a moment. "The meeting is over, gentlemen. Please gather your files there and leave now. Mr. Croome. And you too . . ." He had forgotten the paralegal's name, damn it.

He did not offer his hand to either man. Neither did the others.

Once they left, Alicia came behind Sam and put her arms around his shoulders and held him, her head resting on his back.

Tad folded his arms and nodded at him.

The lights flickered back on.

Sarah is lying on the mattress in her bathroom cell, warmer now because the man had brought her a second blanket after she told him she was cold. She is trying to empty her mind but is not successful. She is exhausting herself worrying about Ricky and now she worries about her parents.

She is the only child. She is everything to them. They are not everything to her. She has her young life, and she has Ricky, and she has, or once thought she had, a long life to live. That's the way it's supposed to work. But her parents, Sam and Donna, have her and only her, their careers coming to a close, their lives approaching decline, her father's memory, especially, losing its acuity, their hopes bound up in Sarah's life and future, and now all of that is blown up.

How are they coping? Do they imagine her dead? Does her mother feel the blood congeal inside her? Does her father rip out his hair in grief and helplessness? Sarah has room for these thoughts because her own fear for herself is manageable.

Sarah remembers the day in the fall of 2017, a year and a half earlier, when she sat on a bench facing Manton Avenue in Providence, eating an egg salad sandwich, and watching two cultures of America collide. It was the day she and Ricky decided to move back to Vermont.

The MAGA-hat boys with their swagger and superiority and laughter, the Guatemalan migrant family with a broken stroller fleeing across the busy avenue in fear. She sees the face of the toddler girl she'd waved to. She hears the wailing mother. She pictures the stroller in the air, as if frozen, then slamming into the pavement, one loose wheel rolling down the street and coming to a stop. The pictures flicker in her mind again and again.

Now she's held in prison by a man wearing a Trump mask. She cannot cross the street. There is no street. She's at his mercy.

The Trump mask stays on, but the two of them have been talking and she finds there is a person behind the mask who has more empathy than the mask or than the person the mask represents. Jack is deep in the MAGA world, but he is trying to understand her. This gives her hope.

When she next hears him moving about the basement, she stands at the door and calls to him. "Hey, Jack?"

"Hold on a second," he replies, and then he appears in the mask at the window. "Yeah?"

"I'm sorry about your father," she begins. "I can see why you're angry about that."

"Yeah, well, it's what you expect."

"Is your mom still around?" Sarah asks.

"Yuh."

"What does she do? Does she work?"

"My mom's a beautician. You know, hair and nails and stuff. She works down to Lebanon." Lebanon is a town about fifteen miles south of Thetford, across the Connecticut River, in New Hampshire.

"Oh good," says Sarah. "Does she like it?"

"She likes it okay. Gets her out of the house, that's the important thing."

"Because it's hard for her to be around your dad?" Sarah asks.

Jack in his mask is silent. She can't see his expression and can't read his mood. "She stays out most evenings too," he says. "Fucking bingo most nights."

Sarah takes a leap. "Does she know what you're doing?"

"What? You mean this thing?"

Sarah nods her head.

"No!"

"Maybe you won't tell her because she'll think it's wrong."

"Jesus, Sarah, I mean what the fuck?" Jack steps away from the window.

"I want to understand, Jack. Come back?" Sarah feels desperate. She can hear him going up the stairs. She sits down on the mattress in misery. She feels dirty and she stands back up and brushes her teeth with the toothbrush and paste he has given her. She tires of doing that and sits again. She hears Jack return and feels relief.

She stands at the little window and speaks out. "You believe everyone should be free. Okay. So how is it you can hold me against my will? How do you square it?"

The mask is there again. "Because," he says, "we've got to make sacrifices to get there."

Sarah hears frustration in his voice.

"My brother says there's a cost to pay to get freedom. You understand? You break eggs to get an omelet, right?"

"Am I the broken egg?" Sarah asks the man.

The mask tilts to the side a hair. They look at each other. She can hear him breathing.

"Jesus, I don't know," he finally utters.

The man leaves, and Sarah is alone again in her cell.

In the action entitled *Sarah Jacobson, et al. v. Second Amendment, Inc.*, Judge Wallis set a date for a status conference in May 2019. In her order, the judge directed the parties to file memoranda addressing the potential impact of *State v. Schenk*, 190 A.3d 820, 2018 VT 45, decided by the Vermont Supreme Court on May 4, 2018, less than a year earlier.

"I think I remember this guy Schenk, who was depositing KKK leaflets on women's doorsteps in Burlington," Sarah told her father and Alicia, as they sat again in the firm's conference room. It was early afternoon on a Thursday in mid-April. They had brought over a large arugula-topped pizza from Pie-R-Squared, just down the block. "But you better remind me what happened in court."

"That's right. William Schenk was a member of the Klan who put leaflets in mailboxes. I should have thought of this case before." Sam passed out paper plates as he spoke. "He was charged with a crime of disorderly conduct under Vermont law, if I recall right. And he was convicted. The ACLU got involved in his appeal; we filed an *amicus* brief in his defense." Sam served on the board of the Vermont chapter of the American Civil Liberties Union.

"The case divided us. Some folks on the board and maybe some on the staff didn't want to get involved in the case. And it likely offended some of our racial justice partners. I should have thought of this case before," he repeated.

Sarah asked how Sam voted.

"You mean, whether the ACLU should join the appeal? Oh, I was in favor. I take the traditional strict First Amendment position. Offensive political speech should be afforded the strongest protection. You might know that decades ago the ACLU infamously sued to protect the rights of Nazis who planned to march in Skokie, Illinois, where many survivors of the Holocaust still lived in the 1970s. This was in that vein.

"And keep in mind the ACLU did not actually represent this guy—William Schenk. The ACLU brief clearly labelled the Klan as a hate group with the most abhorrent ideology. But I don't recall the details now. Alicia, would you?"

Alicia brought a bottle of ginger ale from the mini-fridge. "You pour?" she said to Sam. She had a copy of the *Schenk* opinion in hand and began to turn pages. "It has to do with the disorderly conduct statute, you got that right, Sam, and whether the prosecution proved its case. And the prosecution also sought to enhance the regular penalty by charging him under 13 V.S.A. § 1455, based on the idea that the crime was hate-motivated."

Sam took Title 13 off the shelf and reviewed the statutes.

"Here's what happened," Alicia went on. "Two women in Burlington found flyers advertising the Ku Klux Klan at their homes. One of the women is Mexican American; the other is African American. The flyers were stuck in their mailboxes or jammed somewhere at their front doors. The flyer showed a hooded, robed Klansman mounted on a horse and holding a burning cross."

"Oh my god," said Sarah. "Despicable."

"There's also a Confederate flag on the flyer. Across the top of the flyer, according to the opinion, were the words: *Join the Klan and Save Our Land* followed by four exclamation marks. The bottom of the flyer read *United Northern & Southern Knights of the Ku Klux Klan*. Neither of these women, by the way, noticed this flyer at neighboring homes. And the Burlington police didn't find any other copies either. But a guy who worked at a nearby copy store told the police he'd seen the flyer on one of the store's copy machines.

"The cops viewed surveillance camera footage from the store and were able to identify Schenk. He admitted to distributing the flyers and explained that he is a *Kleagle*—that's apparently a recruiter for the Ku Klux Klan. Schenk told the cops that he had distributed a total of thirty to forty flyers, but I guess that was never established."

Sam asked, "So, no evidence that he was targeting just these two women of color?"

"Right, I guess no definitive evidence either way, at least as presented in the court opinion. Anyway, Schenk was then charged with disorderly conduct, to be specific, that he had"—she quoted—"recklessly created a risk of public inconvenience or annoyance when he engaged in threatening behavior, to wit, by anonymously placing a flyer endorsing the Ku Klux Klan. Plus, he was charged with the hate-motivated sentence enhancement."

Sarah knew enough here to interject. "But unless the flyers were a true threat, like the cross-burning in *Virginia v. Black*, he couldn't be prosecuted because the speech is protected by the First Amendment, right?"

Alicia winked at Sam and said, "The Supreme Court never got there, Sarah. But that is what the parties and the trial court focused on. You're becoming a lawyer, by the way, whether you like it or not. Osmosis at work.

"Schenk's lawyers," she continued, "initially filed a motion to dismiss the charges, arguing that what he did was protected speech under the First Amendment. They argued the flyers did not amount to a true threat, like you said, Sarah. But the trial court didn't buy that. It found that Schenk used the flyers as a tool to convey a strong message of intimidation and to threaten harm. Especially because the women who got the flyer were members of ethnic groups historically targeted for violence by the Klan."

"But the Supreme Court went its own way," Sam said.

"The Supremes reversed," agreed Alicia. "But they ducked the *constitutional* question and instead decided the case on *statutory* grounds. The court took a close look at the disorderly conduct statute and construed it narrowly. The term *threatening behavior* in the statute cannot refer to speech itself, they ruled. You with me? And by speech, they meant to include even things like distributing flyers. Under that statute, distributing flyers cannot amount to threatening *behavior*."

"Okay," said Sarah. "I guess."

Alicia continued the exposition. "The court concluded that leaving flyers at the homes of the two women essentially constituted speech and not nonspeech behavior, and therefore Schenk's actions did not fall under the disorderly conduct statute, which, to repeat, criminalizes only conduct that is not speech. *Voilà*."

"I don't know how plausible that is, trying to make that distinction," argued Sam. "Leaving the flyers in the doors of these women obviously involves speech, but it's conduct too. The court should have avoided the metaphysics and reached the constitutional issue squarely."

The pizza, delicious, was all eaten, and Sam got up to clear the table and wipe it down while Alicia kept talking.

"Well, here's something else, Sam. The court added an alternative route to its result. They held that, even if the statute could be violated by pure speech, the charged conduct would need to convey an *imminent* threat of harm in order to come within the statute's ambit. And they said that was absent in this case. The flyer, they said, is a recruitment solicitation, to get people to join the Klan. I mean, the court is right about that; that's what it really was. There's no explicit statement of threat."

"I really don't get that," said Sarah. "I bet these two women felt threatened. Can you imagine the emotional impact on them?" She checked her phone for the time.

"It's an objective test," said Sam. "But look, in our case, we don't have to rely on the disorderly conduct statute alone as a predicate crime. We can even drop it from the complaint. We can rely on the criminal threatening statute, or stalking, or even extortion, or all of those. Yes? I'm not sure why the good judge is so focused on *Schenk*."

"Perhaps just to narrow the issues."

"And can we establish an imminent threat of serious harm?" said Sam, the skeptic. "What do all those letters actually say?"

He'd read them all before. Alicia retrieved a manila folder from her desk. "First, there was an email to Sarah that said only, *Why are you, a white girl, helping coloreds?* Okay, that is obviously not sufficient by itself. Sarah then gets two more communications. There's a letter left at her apartment door. It says, *I hate you for working for all the colored people trying to replace the American flag.* And then it says this: *Stop coming to the school. Your not wanted. If you don't go we'll make sure you do.*"

Sarah stood and grabbed her backpack. "I have to head out. I . . ."

"Oh god, Sarah, I'm sorry," Alicia interjected. "You don't want to hear these."

"No, no, that's all right. I'm not leaving because of the messages. I really have to go anyway. We have an organizing meeting at Randolph High School this afternoon. Thanks for including me in this. Though it kind of feels like counting angels dancing on a pinhead."

"When's your meeting?" asked her dad.

"It's supposed to start at three o'clock."

"You better get going, Sarahkins." The drive to Randolph took about half an hour.

Alicia bestowed her radiant smile on Sarah and said, "Be well, sweetheart." And Sarah was out the door, on to the next event.

Sam wistfully watched her leave.

"You are a proud dad," Alicia told him, searching for eye contact.

He gave it to her briefly, said only, "That is true," and was back to the case. "That last one you read," Sam said, "*If you don't go we'll make sure you do*, meets the threshold, don't you think?"

"I think it does, Sam, especially when you put them all together. Each message amplifies the others. And there's more. The third one that comes to Sarah is another email. This is the really harsh one. Ready? *Your a little jewish cunt. Patriots will stop what your doing by any means.*" Alicia winced.

She reached out to Sam and put her hand on his shoulder. "I'm sorry, Sam. It's painful to read these." She added, "Like the others, the word *your* is always misspelled the same way, *y-o-u-r*."

Sam sighed deeply. Alicia watched him, imagining his despair at hearing his daughter called a *Jewish cunt*. They looked at each other for a long moment.

He stood and walked carefully to the sink and drank a glass of water. Without turning around, he said, "*Stop what you're doing by any means*. That one sounds like a true threat of serious harm. But does it meet the imminence test? What have we gotta show, for crying out loud?"

"I don't think *Virginia v. Black* itself requires imminence," Alicia noted. "Imminence is required as a statutory element of disorderly conduct under *Schenk*. But we won't rely on that statute. The

First Amendment test in *Virginia v. Black* is whether there is a serious expression of an intent to commit an act of unlawful violence. Imminent or not."

"I see your point," he conceded. "Someone credibly saying *I'm gonna kill you in ten days' time* is uttering a true threat—not protected speech."

Alicia nodded. "That must be right. And Sam, this last email that Sarah got surely meets the test. Then there's the letter Tad got," she continued. "It called him *a dirty jew lawyer*—he's not actually Jewish, by the way, did you know that?—and then it said, *We know what to do with people like you. Garbage people.* That's a threat, the way it invokes Nazi treatment of Jews."

Sam nodded.

"Finally, there's Manny. He got an email that said, *You spic Manny. You make me sick. Go home to Mexico.* Again, you know, by itself it might not suffice. But they are all part of a pattern."

"A course of conduct," said Sam, "that might indict Marty Frazier. We've still got to tie it to the national organization."

One of the Randolph High School organizers texted Sarah, as the meeting had begun and Sarah had not yet arrived. There was no reply.

Ah well, thought the organizer, not everyone's reliable. She sent another text forty-five minutes later and then let it be.

At a meeting later the same day, Tad explained the settlement options to the school superintendent, Sherise Bailey, and the school board chair, Allen Dahlbert. "He offers to dismiss the appeal if the school district pays the sum of $40,000. One might perhaps argue that this can largely be characterized as nuisance money, because responding to the appeal—writing our briefs, oral argument in the City, and so forth—will cost a significant sum."

"I hate to pay them a penny," said Sherise. "Racist bastards. I'm sorry, someone's got to say it."

"I understand," Tad said. "I feel this way as well. It is probably wise, however, not to rest too much on principle. I suggest we might come back to them with an offer of $5,000 and see what transpires."

Allen asked Tad what sort of risk they faced in the appeal.

"My view, frankly," Tad offered, "is that this was a close case. The law is not yet so finely tuned on this subject. Hence, yes, we do face risk that the lower court's judgment will be overturned. I cannot quantify it for you."

"The board meets tomorrow evening. I'll make sure we include an executive session on the agenda to discuss ongoing litigation. You can attend, Tad?"

"Certainly," replied the lawyer. "It would be helpful, I think, to ask the board for authorization to spend a sum of up to, say, $30,000 in order to settle the litigation. By the way, this gentleman Gerald Croome is, how shall I put it, truly an asshole."

Sherise laughed. "I've never heard you speak that way about anyone, Tad. And certainly not by using language like that."

"Yes, I suppose that is so. I save such choice descriptions only for occasions when they are truly warranted."

Ricky, who now worked as a tutor for two boys with special needs at the elementary school in Montpelier, came home as usual at about 3:30 and changed into his running clothes. He figured Sarah would be late getting home because of her meeting at the Randolph High School.

It was April and still cold in Vermont, so he wore sweatpants and a windbreaker as he headed up North Street. As always, the steep climb was brutal, and he took perverse pleasure in punishing himself for his life's misdeeds. In that one respect, he was much like Sarah's father Sam, who always said he had few good memories and harbored only regrets about the past.

The road turned to dirt at the top of the hill. The ice that had packed into the dirt over the winter had thawed and the road here was now composed of clay mud, channeled into ruts by passing cars.

Ricky ran along the edge of the road where the surface was firmer. This time, he kept going beyond Goodman Road on the right and Sparrow Farm Road on the left, into the thick woods another mile or more to where it came to a T at Horn of the Moon Road. The tiny frogs known as peepers were just beginning their evening shrill chant as he passed the marshy areas along the road— not yet reaching their crescendo of deafening madness.

Ricky's long legs found a lovely rhythm along this stretch in the woods, his breathing slowed, and the peepers enchanted him. Ricky smiled as he thought how Sarah made fun of what she called his zen state of mind. He was in it now.

On Horn of the Moon, he turned left, leaving the woods behind as the road rolled down through open pastures to a grand view of the Abenaki Range. His stride lengthened here, and he wondered if Sarah were home by now, and he could hardly wait to see her open, sweet face and he would cook a nice meal for them, using the polenta he had prepared the day before and the mushrooms in the fridge, and maybe they would have a glass of wine together. Then maybe they would lie together in bed, naked under the covers, and he could touch her skin and massage her small and perfect breasts, and she might reach down and stroke him for a minute and then move on top of him while he lay on his back as their lips and noses pressed against each other.

Ricky reached Jacobs Road and took another left, next to the old barn that the light filtered through, and began another long uphill climb over muddy ruts. He worked harder here, and it brought him back to earth from his sexual reverie. He loved Sarah. He knew she loved him equally but at the same time differently because she also loved others.

He remembered how she had talked about Tyrene, her boy-friend in Providence who had been killed in 2015, how he had inspired her, how strongly she felt she loved him, how he had pushed her away and hurt her, and how she had hurt him back.

Ricky never met Tyrene. But he closely studied the few photographs of him that Sarah had printed and kept in a pile on her dresser: Tyrene staring into the camera lens with a penetrating frown; Tyrene walking arm in arm with Sarah on the Brown campus; Tyrene looking, Ricky admitted, stunningly handsome. It didn't matter to Ricky. Sarah's heart had expansive capacity. There was room for him.

Jacobs Road came out on Sparrow Farm Road, where a third left turn and another mile or so along the last arm of the lopsided rectangle brought him back to North Street, first passing by the farm with the long-haired, long-horned cattle. Just two or three miles more down the hill to the center of town.

He got home at 6:30 and was surprised to find no one home. And no message.

He felt a little queasy. He dawdled for a bit, then took a shower.

He called Sarah's cell, but her phone seemed to be dead. He knew there was cell service in Randolph, even if not in the towns nearby. He called Donna and Sam. They hadn't heard from her either. Queasiness turned into fear, and he was having trouble thinking clearly.

He tried a general number at the Randolph High School and, not surprisingly for this hour, reached a voice mail system.

He called Donna back. Neither of them knew who to call, who might be connected with the Randolph organizing meeting. Ricky found a landline number for Samantha Janey, BLM's coordinator, and spoke to someone he assumed was a boyfriend. He told Ricky Samantha was out and, once Ricky explained who he was and why he was calling, he gave Ricky Samantha's cell number.

Ricky finally connected with Samantha, but she didn't know much about the Randolph meeting or who was involved either. She was surprisingly unhelpful, and Ricky was now feeling angry. What the fuck, what kind of a fucking organization doesn't protect its organizers?

He didn't say these things to Samantha.

Ricky called Donna back again. They decided Ricky would drive to Randolph to see what he could find out before involving police. Ricky borrowed Donna's car.

"Please drive safely," Donna said. She hugged him hard.

In Randolph, Ricky called Donna on his cell phone. "The school is locked up," he said. "No one is around. I can't see her car anywhere." What had he really expected?

Donna talked with Sam for a moment. Then she told Ricky, "We're going to call the state police and report this. I'll call Barry LaPorte too. All right? Oh, Ricky. You come back here. Don't go home to an empty house."

Darkness settled around him. Darkness settled within him.

Tad Sorowski and Gerald Croome spent considerable effort to negotiate a settlement of the BLM flag case. To Tad's dismay, he did find himself in the gutter, nickel and diming his way through the process of carving up the difference between a demand of $40,000 and the school board's counteroffer of $5,000.

In the end, they arrived at the figure of $20,000, probably predictable from the start, as the amount to be paid to the family of student Collin Chapman and the Second Amendment organization in exchange for dismissal of their Second Circuit appeal and a release of all claims relating to the BLM flag.

The upshot was that the federal district court's decision on the motion to dismiss in favor of the school, issued by Judge Wallis, remained the final word. The Black Lives Matter flag could fly, and U-32 was not required to fly anyone else's flag on the school's flagpole.

It was a legal victory for the U-32 school and the students who'd organized to display their power and pride in the movement for racial justice. And best of all, Tad Sorowski believed the decision would stand as precedent throughout Vermont, and even beyond Vermont's borders.

But he could not celebrate. He was in regular communication with Ricky Stillwell and Sarah's parents. There was no word about Sarah. No news, in this case, was bad news.

Then news did come. Alicia found a letter that had been pushed through the mail slot in her office. The envelope bore only the printed words *Mr. Jacobson*. Inside, on a single sheet of paper, were words printed in block letters:

> HELLO MR. JACOBSON. WE HAVE SARA AND SHE IS SAFE. WE WILL GIVE HER BACK TO HER FAMILY BUT YOU HAVE TO DO 2 THINGS. YOU HAVE TO DISMISS THE LEGAL SUIT AGAINST SECOND AMENDMENT. IT HAS TO BE DONE WITH PREDJEDISE. THE SECOND THING IS TO PAY US 50,000 DOLLARS IN CASH IN SMALL BILLS (20S AND 50S) THAT ARE OLD AND USED. WHEN I HAVE PROOF OF THE FIRST THING (DISMISSAL OF LEGAL CASE), I WILL SEND INSTRUCTIONS ABOUT THE MONEY.

In her cell in the basement, Sarah listens to the man, who has just brought her yogurt and orange juice, from which she deduces this is breakfast and it must be morning. He asks her what else he can get her and adds, "I want you to be happy."

Maybe he says that because she has been crying for some time, although she thought she was keeping it to herself.

She is tempted to say, "Are you fucking crazy? You kidnapped me and you're holding me in a prison cell, and you want me to be happy?" Instead, she smiles weakly at the Trump mask and says, "I know that, Jack. The way to make me happy is to let me go. Please?"

"I can't do that now," he says. "We've got to wait longer and see what happens with everything. But I'm treating you right, aren't I?"

On Friday night, Ricky returned to the Jacobsons' house on Adams Street. He went there for comfort, and he found some with Sam and Donna, who were equally stunned by fear and anger and sorrow. Shared commiseration helped a bit. But reality was bleak.

The police had no leads. They had pressed Marty Frazier to no avail. Barry LaPorte told them he thought Marty was not part of the kidnapping. As for the ransom note, the FBI specialists were working on a plan, they said, and would talk with them soon.

Alicia swung by in the morning to give whatever support she could. They all sat at the kitchen table and drank coffee. There was nothing much useful to say.

Alicia tried to prompt Donna to come to a workout with her, a spinning class on stationary bicycles at the fitness studio on Sproul Street.

"I don't think so, Alicia," Donna said. "I don't like gyms. But thank you for asking."

Gyms. A memory was triggered deep in Ricky's mind. "Wait," he said, and the expectant look on his unshaved face drew them all in.

"I'm not sure of this. It's probably not helpful. It's just that I remember something from last year." Ricky could feel Alicia's leg vibrating under the table. She was always a bit impatient with his pace. "I went to a meeting at someone's house on Sherman Street. It was part of SURJ, you know the group?"

"Yup, know the group. What happened?"

He was thinking it out. "We were asked to talk with another person in the room, to share an experience we'd had where we had confronted the issue of race in some way, and how we responded to it. I paired up with someone. I remember his name was Joe. Joe told me a story about meeting someone at a gym who had been to Charlottesville and was in the white supremacy march."

"And?"

"And the guy Joe met there at the gym said something awful about Jews and Communists to Joe. And the other key thing is that Joe said this guy was a lawyer, I think in Burlington, but I'm not sure about that part."

"The guy who had been in Charlottesville was a lawyer?"

"Right. That I do remember, but I don't know about the Burlington part."

"And you think maybe this white supremacist lawyer guy might have something to do with Sarah's kidnapping?"

Ricky nodded slightly. "All the obsession with Jews, you know? Like in the messages. It sounded similar."

"Do we know his name?" Sam asked the question.

"No."

"How can we get in touch with Joe?" Alicia asked.

Just then Alicia's phone rang. She answered. "Oh, hi Barry," she said, walking into the study off the kitchen. She listened for a long minute, interrupting only once with a question. The others watched Alicia as she returned frowning. "I'll pass it along. I'm with them now." She thanked Barry and hung up.

"Barry says they found Sarah's car." Ricky, Donna, and Sam took this in, their spirits visibly diminished further. "It was at the commuter parking lot near Randolph, next to Exit 4 on the highway. He says a state trooper who checks the lot periodically noticed the car because it hadn't been moved for 36 hours. So he called in the license number."

"Shit," said Ricky. Donna and Sam clutched each other's hands.

Donna asked, "Did they learn anything useful from the car?"

"Sorry, no, nothing obvious. Nothing left inside the car, except a folder of Sarah's papers in the back seat. They'll check for prints and analyze it for fibers and stuff."

Alicia turned to Ricky. "What about this Joe guy? How can we find him?"

"I don't know. I don't know his last name. I don't know where he lives. But listen, the organizer or the host of this meeting was a woman named Eleanor Mandell. But I don't even know whose house it was."

"Oh, I know Eleanor," said Alicia. "She's a mediator."

"She goes to the Unitarian Church," Ricky added.

"You're a champ, Ricky," Alicia said, flashing her beautiful warm smile.

Alicia called Eleanor Mandell. A machine answered. Alicia left a message. "I'm going to the office," she told the others. "I'm going to follow up, okay? You hang in."

Alicia left. Sam muttered, "I'm useless."

When they finally connected, Eleanor tried to be helpful. "Yes, Alicia. I remember that meeting on Sherman Street. It was the only one we had up in the college neighborhood. I even remember some of the conversation. It was a better meeting than some. And yes," she said, when prompted, "I remember Ricky being there. And who's the other person you're asking about?"

"Someone called Joe."

"I don't think so." There was a pause. "I don't remember everyone who came to the meeting, although I do remember Ricky was there, because I know Ricky from church, and he's been coming to other meetings. I always admire how he speaks his mind. He's got a lot of courage, that young man."

Alicia was impatient, as usual. "But not Joe?"

"I don't recall anyone by that name at that meeting. But listen, Alicia. We always have a contact list that we circulate around at the SURJ conversations."

"That's awesome," Alicia said. "Do you have the lists? How can we get it?"

"The problem is, we don't keep the actual lists."

"Well, fuck," said Alicia.

"What we do," replied Eleanor with equanimity, "is I or Peter enter the data in an Excel file when we get around to it. That would have been done here. Let me see what I can find out. Let me call you back in a bit."

"Hurry?" pleaded Alicia.

Alicia waited. She checked her emails. She replied to a client's inquiry about a grievance procedure. She waited.

Eleanor called back. "I've got the spreadsheet up on my screen. There's only one Joseph, Joseph Shepard. Is that who you're looking for?"

Alicia knew Joseph Shepard. "Oh no, because I'm sure Ricky knows Joseph, and he would have told me that's who it was."

Eleanor said, "And I know he wasn't at that meeting anyway. It could be this other Joe never put his information on the clipboard list that was used that evening. Really, I have no idea."

"Thanks anyway," said Alicia, hanging up and stewing. It's not even Joe I'm trying to find, she thought.

She called Ricky, as she had promised. "Eleanor doesn't know who Joe is, Ricky. She doesn't have any record of him at the meeting. I'm sorry."

Ricky took this in and said, "I remember something else. Both Joe and the guy he talked with at the gym had shaved heads."

Alicia kept thinking about the horror of Charlottesville that evening. She was home, in the old farmhouse up on Bull Riley Road. Barb was out for the evening with her women's book group. They were reading a mystery written by a local author, Susan Ritz.

Alicia opened her laptop and googled "Charlottesville riots." She explored some sites and settled on YouTube videos of Nazis and the Klan marching in Charlottesville. There they were, carrying torches, chanting "YOU WILL NOT REPLACE US. JEWS WILL NOT REPLACE US."

How idiotic, how gross. Young men, all men, holding Confederate flags and torches, chanting in the deep voice adolescent boys sometimes affect to sound more mature than they really are. Many with shaved heads. She could barely look and felt sick to her stomach. Yet she persisted.

She was watching the third video when something caught her eye. Alicia thought she recognized a face in the crowd belonging to a marcher with a shaved head and a full blond beard, one of the stupid, sweating, chanting faces, many of them looking more or less alike. It was dark and the faces were eerily lit by the torches. The face appeared for a half-second before being obscured by another body. The face then reappeared briefly.

Alicia watched it again.

"Are you home?" she asked Donna, who had answered the phone. It was late but not too late. "Is Ricky still there?" The answer was yes. "Can I come over now? I'm also going to see if Barry can come. There is something."

Alicia left a brief note for her wife and took off, arriving breathless at Donna's house. She pulled out her laptop. "Let me check something first," she said. She found the website for the law office, Shelby & Croome. One page included photographs of the dozen lawyers at the firm. Below that were photos of three paralegals. "There," she said, pointing.

"That's the guy in the suit who was at the conference in our office a couple of weeks ago," said Sam. "Weird guy. Built like a truck."

"And who also was at the court hearing last fall," Alicia added. "His name is Keith Thomas. Now look at this."

Alicia pulled up the YouTube video, fast-forwarded to the right place, then slowed it to normal speed. "There," she said, stopping the video.

Ricky gasped. "Him? That's him?"

"It looks like it might be the same guy," said Sam. "With a full beard, though. Hard to tell."

"I'm sure of it now," said Alicia.

"Croome's paralegal was marching at Charlottesville," Sam mused. "What does it mean?"

Barry LaPorte knocked on the door and was let in. The demonstration was repeated. The questions were repeated.

"It kind of looks like the same person," said Barry. "The beard makes it hard to compare."

"Like I said," said Sam.

Barry said, "Look, I've got more new information to share." He cleared his throat. "It's not very good news. We took a look at the surveillance video at the service station next to Exit 4, from Thursday. We figured just in case, because it's so close to the commuter parking area up there where they found Sarah's Honda. It shows Sarah pulling in next to the gas pumps."

"Oh!" exclaimed Donna.

"She doesn't get out of the car though. Then you can see a man approach the car, walking rapidly, and he gets in the car, the rear door. He's got a red and black coat on and wears a baseball cap pulled low over his eyes. Plus, he sort of holds his arm over his face, like he knows about the surveillance cameras. Then they drive off. That's it."

Ricky's head hung down.

Donna stared at Barry.

Sam asked, "Can you tell if it's this guy, what's his name?"

"Keith Thomas," says Alicia.

"In the surveillance video? No, I don't think so. I mean, I don't think you can tell one way or the other. The man in the video is well-built too, but that's about all. It looks like he's clean-shaven, but you can't really see his face. He's wearing dark glasses. And the quality of the video is very poor."

Alicia asked Barry, "Do we have enough for a search warrant of Thomas's home or whatever properties he has? Or to bring him in for questioning?"

"God damn it, I don't know." Barry thought a bit. "Let me bring this to Ed Duffy at the FBI and see what he says. I'll check with the state police too. I'll move quickly. We may need you to make out an affidavit, Alicia."

Alicia asked, "The Feds have an interest at this point?"

"Yup, because Second Amendment used the mails and wired funds between states. It triggers possible federal crimes. At least that's the situation for Marty Frazier, the guy who sent those emails. But we don't really know whether there's any connection between what happened here and the national organization."

Keith Thomas owned a one-bedroom condo in Winooski and no other real estate in his name. When they knew he wasn't home, the FBI conducted a quiet search. It was a Sunday, three days after Sarah disappeared.

The warrant was limited to evidence of kidnapping, essentially what was in plain view. The agents were not permitted to search through papers or even to open drawers or containers. The condo was neat, well-organized. There was no art on the walls. The few books on a shelf included some economics and legal textbooks, Ayn Rand fiction, a book called *The Camp of the Saints*. On the kitchen counter, where some mail sat in a pile, there was an envelope from the National Rifle Association in view. They honored the warrant's limitations and did not disturb the pile. In fact, they disturbed nothing and left no trace of their presence in the condo. They found nothing to suggest that Sarah had been held there.

Ricky didn't take the news well. He was disintegrating. When he wasn't at the Jacobsons' house, he mostly stayed home in his Sproul Street apartment, avoiding people, avoiding news of the world. He was granted a medical leave of absence from work. He stopped running. He didn't eat very well. Pie-R-Squared Pizza was a few doors away. Their two-slices-and-a-beer special sustained him, as far as it went.

Alicia knocked at Ricky's door around noon on the day after the search. "Will you join me for a bit?" she asked. "I've got an appointment at 12:30 for my car, for an oil change and inspection at this garage in Barre where I go. They said it'll take a couple hours and I want to bring you to this cool new vegetarian restaurant. Please?"

Ricky agreed. He wasn't speaking much, but his mood was calmed by being with Alicia. She didn't ask him how he was doing.

They left her car at the garage and walked to the new restaurant. They ate and drank coffee and talked about this and that; the point was just to be together and put on a show of doing normal things.

They joked about the name of the place, Five Tees. Neither knew what it signified. Alicia: "It stands for Tofu, Tempeh, Tahini, and . . . not sure of the others." Ricky: "Tabouleh!" Alicia: "Right, and Tamari." Ricky: "Tortellini!" Alicia: "Okay, that makes six. Also, they don't have tortellini." Ricky: "Taxidermy!" Alicia: "What?"

She beamed at him. Ricky, so desperate and distraught, smiled back. They had more coffee and ordered two huge, healthy cookies for dessert.

Returning to the garage, Ricky waited with Alicia in line behind a few customers at the service desk. Everybody's car needed repairs, more that day than most it seemed. The customer at the front of the line was talking with the technician at the counter about hybrid cars. They were taking too long.

The customer was then saying something about how he used to drive a Mustang. "I was kinda crazy back then," he told the technician.

Ricky was suddenly startled into attention. And now he realized the customer had a shaved head. Ricky sprang forward and to the side, so he could see the man's face. He jolted and spoke too loudly: "Joe!"

"Oh, hey, how you doin', man?"

"I'm Ricky Stillwell, remember? I need to talk with you, Joe. It's an emergency. Please."

"Okay, sure, can I just finish up with this?" He did so, and Ricky pulled him aside and tried to explain. Alicia begged the other two customers if she could move to the front of the line and they agreed. Joe heard Ricky out and said he'd rush to Montpelier and meet them at Alicia's office.

They sat in front of the computer screen while Alicia pulled up the Charlottesville video, advanced it to the spot and let it play for a few seconds, then stopped it. "Do you see the guy there with the shaved head and beard, right there?" She pointed at the frozen screen.

"This guy?" said Joe. "I don't know. I don't think he's the same person that I saw at the gym. Dammit, these skinheads look alike."

Ricky dropped his head down to the level of his knees. He moaned. "We've got to do something."

"But wait," said Joe, still peering closely at the screen. "Play a few seconds of it running, would you?" Joe watched. "Next to your guy? Walking next to him? Same shaved head, same bushy beard. He comes in and out of view. That's him."

Ricky bounced up. "That's him? You're sure? That's the same person you saw in the gym who told you he was a lawyer?"

"Yuh, pretty sure."

Alicia replayed the video for several frames. "Look at that," she said. "These two guys look really similar. I bet they're brothers."

Through Barry LaPorte's efforts as intermediary, FBI Special Agent Duffy confirmed that Keith Thomas, Croome's paralegal, had a brother, one year younger, named Kyle. Kyle was presently unemployed, having previously worked in auto parts sales and as a mechanic. He owned a home on a back road two miles from Thetford Center, a small Vermont village near the Connecticut River, an hour southeast from Montpelier.

The same Monday afternoon, about 4:00 p.m., the same magistrate judge issued another warrant. A similar team assembled. They drove for close to a mile up the gravel road in two unmarked cars, not wanting to alert anyone they might encounter along the narrow road. Kyle lived in a geodesic dome he had constructed from a kit on a twenty-acre tract of wooded land, just beyond the property that once was home to the Town of Thetford's poor farm.

The agents parked on the edge of the road and walked up the drive. Next to the dome was a big shed that appeared to be used as a workshop. Various pieces of equipment, in various states of repair, were strewn around the front and side of the shed. Beneath the overhang on one side of the shed was a store of firewood. Uncut logs were piled nearby. On the other side of the logs were a Ford pickup and an old Camaro dating back to the '70s.

A man emerged from the house and stood on the flagstone step below the door. He was solidly built, an old plaid flannel shirt tight on his chest and shoulders. He stepped back in the house and came out a second later with a rifle. "The fuck you want?" he told the cops, who now had their hands on their holsters.

FBI Agent Duffy introduced himself and explained the warrant to search the premises. As he did so, two agents went into the shed. "Anyone else here?" Duffy inquired.

"No one's here," the man yelled. "You can't come in. It's my own home. Get those guys out of my workshop." He started to raise the rifle.

Duffy called out, "Stop! You point that thing at us, and we will shoot you dead. You want that?" Agents now pointed their guns at the man.

The man hesitated, the rifle in his right hand, halfway into a shooting position.

Duffy yelled, "Drop the rifle! Now!"

The man froze, his mouth open. He didn't drop the rifle. He turned his head to watch the men emerging from the shed and as he did so, the arm holding the rifle came up.

Duffy spoke urgently. "Hit his arms."

Two officers fired their weapons and the man screamed, the rifle clattering to the flagstone. The agents rushed him and pinned him to the ground. One strapped his legs; another called for medical assistance.

"Shoot me, fucking shoot me, kill me!" growled Kyle Thomas.

An agent, with bizarre courtesy, said, "We can't do that, sir."

Another pushed the front door ajar and peered cautiously inside. Then they heard a muted yell from inside the dome.

Part IV

The Wrong Place in Life

The first evening, Sarah and Ricky held each other in bed very quietly. But she soon felt she had to move, so they went out at midnight for a walk around the familiar streets of Montpelier.

Sarah's internal clock was all off. She was amazed to learn she had been captive for only four days and nights.

Ricky held her hand as they strolled and told the story of their anxious efforts to find her. They stood on the bridge over the Scape River and listened to the water rush over the dam, then came back on Sproul Street, past the clothing boutiques, the noodle shop, the taco shop, Bear Pond Books, and Charlie-O's Tavern, now closed because it was a Monday night.

They turned left on Chamber. No one else was on the street. Past the kitchenware store, past Jacobson & Santana Law Offices, past Wilaiwan's Kitchen on the left and Sacred Grounds on the right, past the courthouse, and on to the green in front of the grand Statehouse. They huddled on a bench for a few minutes until the cold set in their bones, then they walked back to their apartment. Sarah told him she was all right.

The next morning, Tuesday, her parents picked up hot biscuits, some plain, some with egg and cheese, at Down Home Kitchen, where Mary Alice, the proprietor, insisted they take them without paying. "Not after what y'all have been through," she said.

They now gathered around the small table in the apartment on Sproul Street above the hardware store. Ricky had made coffee to serve with the gifted hot biscuits. They were all pouring love into Sarah.

"I know it's been worse for you all. *Really*," she emphasized as they shook their heads in disbelief. "For me, I was there every moment. I knew I wasn't dead. I knew I wasn't hurt. I wasn't even scathed."

"Thank god," murmured Ricky.

"Here is what it was like for me." She wanted them to understand. "I didn't know what could happen in the next moment, and then the next—but I knew what each moment that passed held. But you all"—Sarah made a shrugging gesture and looked around at her parents and Ricky—"you didn't have the benefits I had. You didn't know what I knew."

She looked at Ricky beseechingly. His face was lined with so much pain, she had to turn away. She felt responsible for them and felt she had to draw them back into the normalities of daily life. She asked, "Can I eat one of those now?"

"But Sarah," said her father, as he handed her a biscuit on a plate. "You must have been terrified." He passed her the butter, a knife, and a napkin.

"Yes, I was scared, all the time," said Sarah, "and lonely, of course. But there was something a bit pathetic about the man— Kyle Thomas, I guess he's called?—because he started being sweet to me in his strange way."

"Sweet cannot be the right word for this," said Ricky.

"No, no, he really was. He tried to bring me foods I liked. And then he started to call me *Sarah*. He called me by my name."

"He gave you back some dignity, maybe?" Donna finally spoke.

"It made a huge difference to me. He wanted to please me, like the way he brought me to the shower, I think it was twice. I can't really put it all in proper sequence."

Ricky imagined the man in the Trump mask taking Sarah to the shower. He ground his teeth and shook his head, sickened by the images. He looked at Donna and Sam in turn, to gauge how they reacted. Donna looked puzzled.

Sam glanced back at Ricky with a hideous grimace. "Stockholm," Sam spat out.

"No, Dad, don't be dumb, not that." She was used to her father saying stupid things. "I'm just trying to tell you how it actually felt. I think I'm okay. And, so you know, he gave me privacy in the shower."

"I started to imagine—" Donna began.

"Mom!?"

"—I started to imagine writing your obituary."

"Oh, sweetheart," said Sam.

"Sarah Jacobson's life," Donna recited, "was cut short by a man with the face of Donald Trump, because of her work . . ."

"No, Donna, come on." Sam reached for and held Donna's hand.

". . . because of her good work for racial justice." She added, "Her good trouble."

They sat at the table silently.

"Oh Mom," said Sarah.

"I felt proud of you," Donna said.

The doorbell chimed. Sam said, "I told you, didn't I, that I told Alicia and Barb they could come over for a bit?" Ricky didn't think Sam had mentioned this before. "They just really wanted to see you."

Ricky buzzed them up. With Alicia and Barb also arrived Tad Sorowski, who happened to be looking for the right entrance to the building when Alicia and Barb appeared. Ricky welcomed them all in. Sam said apologetically to Ricky, "I might have invited Tad too. Did I tell you?"

Ricky stood at the counter and brewed another pot. The ones who had just arrived surrounded Sarah. Tad was reserved compared to the others, who did not want to stop touching and kissing their Sarah. But even Tad was teary in his joy at seeing Sarah here in the living flesh.

The breakfast biscuits were passed around.

"I'd like to understand it better," Sarah said, when the opportunity arose. She turned towards Alicia. "I hear you were looking through photos from the Charlottesville riot and you spotted the paralegal—the one who was in court with Gerald Croome? Fucking amazing."

She realized as she said the word *fucking* that it was a way to show her parents she wasn't damaged. Her word choice wasn't premeditated, but it was deliberate. Neither was it false bravado. So she repeated it. "Really fucking amazing." She experienced a touch of giddiness.

Donna did not use words like that herself, but she understood instinctively what Sarah was conveying. Donna laughed out loud, she too feeling a touch giddy.

"It was Ricky," Alicia explained, "who made the connection. He was at a meeting a couple of years ago, one of the SURJ neighborhood meetings, and he remembered someone at the meeting telling a story about having met a man who had been marching in Charlottesville."

"It was just a year ago, Alicia," said Ricky.

"Ricky told me that," Sarah said. "There was someone called Joe, who'd met one of the neo-Nazi marchers. But I'm still confused about how you all put it together."

"Here's what happened," said Alicia. "At the SURJ meeting, there was a man called Joe who told Ricky about having met the Nazi guy. The Nazi guy had said he was a lawyer. And Joe also said the guy talked about Jewish scum or something like that. It sounded an awful lot like the letters and emails that you got. So maybe, we thought, maybe there was a connection between him and Marty Frazier. Maybe this self-styled lawyer who hated Jews and spoke that way might be involved in your, you know, disappearance.

"We first tried to find Joe, hoping he could give us a lead, but Ricky didn't know his last name and we didn't know where to find him. Then I figured I should scan over the video shot at Charlottesville. Who knows what I'd find? And, yeah, I recognized Croome's paralegal, Keith Thomas, in some of the video."

"Doesn't surprise me," said Sam, "that Keith Thomas would tell people he was a lawyer. The big shit in his fancy suit trying to elevate his status."

"But no," said Alicia, "it wasn't Keith Thomas who said that. He's not the one Joe had met, boasting about being at Charlottesville."

"Oh, right," Sam agreed. "Finish the story, Alicia."

"So we recognized Keith Thomas in the video. And then the feds searched Keith's house, up in Winooski, and found nothing. So, we were crushed. You were missing, Sarah, and we were freaking out. I don't know how we all kept it together." Alicia nodded her head towards Sam and Donna and Ricky. "At some point we got the stupid ransom letter. You saw that?"

"No, I don't think so. Not then, not at the cabin, or dome, or whatever it was. Who lives in a dome?"

"No, I mean did you see the letter now?"

"Ricky, did you show me what she's talking about?"

"No, I didn't show it. I don't even have a copy."

"Okay," said Alicia. "Then a miraculous thing happened. Like I said, we hadn't been able to find Joe."

"Joe from the SURJ meeting."

"Right, Sarah," said Ricky. "I'd only met him that once, at the SURJ meeting last year. I didn't get his full name then. Now we know he's Joe McCracken. Lives in Barre."

"After the dead-end search of Keith's place in Winooski," Alicia picked up the narrative again, "Ricky and I happened to be in Barre taking my car for service at a garage. We're standing at the desk waiting our turn behind people, and Ricky looks at the man in front of us and it's him, it's Joe. No shit. This is totally serendipitous. Joe comes back with us and looks at the same video, tells us Keith Thomas is not the person he met at the gym."

"Sorry, what's this about a gym?" interrupted Sarah.

Ricky clarified: "Joe told me that it was at a gym where he met the Nazi guy. The gym's not important."

"We show the Charlottesville video to Joe," Alicia continued. "He watches it again, and he sees the person he'd met at the gym marching right *next* to Keith Thomas. His lookalike brother. Your kidnapper, Kyle Thomas."

"He worked out in a gym," Sarah mused. "Yeah, I can see that."

"And guess what," Alicia said, "the FBI knows Kyle lives by himself in a geodesic dome in the woods in Thetford Center."

"A dome plopped over a full basement, with its own bathroom. I called him Jack, you know." She paused a moment. "But he isn't a lawyer, is he?"

"No," said Alicia. "I guess he just made that up. Who knows why."

"To feel like a player," Sam interjected. "To be better than his brother. To impress."

"He really didn't hurt you?" asked Donna.

A couple of days later, Sarah felt ready for a visit with her friends on the board—Samantha, Elena, and Chip. She decided she would like to get out of the apartment, and they agreed to meet at the bagel shop at the end of Sproul Street near the Scape River. Ricky was reluctant to join.

"I got pretty mad at Samantha the night you disappeared," he explained. "I didn't tell you before. She wasn't helpful when I was trying to find out what happened to you."

"Oh Ricky. I'm so sorry. Did you share that with Samantha?"

"Oh god, no. I wouldn't."

"Well then, would you please come with me?"

Sarah and Ricky walked into the bagel shop. Sarah was immediately surrounded and held in loving embraces. Samantha pulled out of the huddle and turned to Ricky. "You're Ricky?"

"Yes. Are you Samantha?"

"That's me!" She brought him away from the others and she guided him to an empty booth. "Listen, I felt so awful after you called me that evening when Sarah didn't come home from Randolph. I was completely helpless and didn't give you any support and I realized afterwards how totally overwhelmed and devastated you must have been. I've been killing myself."

Ricky was contrite. "Oh, Samantha, I don't know that there was anything you could have done."

"But weren't you pissed at me? Please be honest. I was useless."

"Honest? Okay, I guess I was at my wit's end and needed someone to blame for what happened. I blamed you in that moment. You were not to blame. Of course, I know that."

Samantha reached out and put her hand on Ricky's arm. They sat like that for some time and did not shy away from looking directly at each other.

"Shit, Samantha, you're making me cry," said Ricky.

"I know," she said.

"And I don't even know you."

"But I think we're friends already, Ricky Stillwell."

"You know my last name?"

"Yes, I do. Mine's Janey. So nice to meet you."

Elena sidled up to the booth, looked at them with interest, and said, "You each want a bagel? Tell me what kind and I'll make the order."

"Elena," said Samantha, "have you met Ricky? Sure, would you place an order for me for an everything bagel, toasted with veggie cream cheese, plus a large coffee?"

"For you, Ricky?"

"Thank you, but I'm going to sit and think about it for a minute. I'm not sure yet."

The Montpelier city councilor, the Norwich legislator, and one of the other student members of the GMBLM board arrived about this time. A celebratory spirit filled the bagel shop. Ricky sat in the booth and smiled at everyone.

Marty Frazier, the True Patriots' enthusiast, was indeed a dumb fuck, as Kyle Thomas, also arguably a dumb fuck, had called him. After Barry LaPorte had taken his phone as evidence, Frazier had gone out and purchased another and was back in communication with Neil Davison at Second Amendment headquarters in Richmond, Virginia, and with Kyle Thomas and his brother Keith, the paralegal at the Croome law firm. But there was nothing about the kidnapping plot in the communications with Frazier.

It was a search of Kyle Thomas's computer that produced emails, not synched to his phone account, that cemented the deal. His brother Keith had sent an email to Davison in late March with the subject line *Approval for SJ Snatch?* It was copied to Kyle. In the text of the email, Keith wrote:

> Kyle is ready to snatch SJ. He's got plans and a safe place to put her. Somewhere in the fucking woods no one will find her. It's a good plan and they can get the case thrown out of court. We're putting our money into expenses and want to know about being paid back. Kyle's waiting for the right moment for the snatch. Need your okay to proceed.

Davison replied:

> Very good. Go forward with snatch. Submit invoices for legit expenses. Keep Marty totally out of the loop. Charlottesville isn't over. Delete these emails.

Kyle Thomas followed the first command; he completed the snatch. Keith Thomas followed the second command to submit the invoices; the officers found a trail of invoices and payments. The Thomas brothers presumably followed the third command and did not share their plans with Marty Frazier.

Luckily for the cops and the plaintiffs, Kyle had ignored the last directive. It appeared he didn't delete anything. The messages remained on his Gmail account.

The FBI raided the Second Amendment, Inc. offices in Virginia and got a court order to seize their financial assets, including a bank account with over $30,000 in cash and an investment account with securities valued just under $900,000.

In Vermont, Judge Mildred Wallis scheduled an expedited hearing, at which she granted Alicia's request for an order attaching the assets for the benefit of the plaintiffs. Over the next couple of weeks, Alicia had several phone calls and meetings with her clients, interspersed with spirited negotiation sessions with Gerald Croome.

At Sarah and Ricky's apartment, Alicia outlined the broad terms of the negotiation. "Second Amendment will turn over all their funds and they will close shop." She had her hand on Sarah's arm. "We shut them down, Sarah."

Sarah grabbed Alicia's hand. "You mean it?"

"I mean it."

Sarah pulled her into a bear hug, then pulled back and looked at Alicia thoughtfully. "Why would they agree? What are they getting out of it?"

"They don't have a lot of room to maneuver. What they get is that we would give up any claim to go after the individuals associated with this outfit, to go after them personally. This is what lawyers call the consideration for the deal."

"Punish the monkey and let the organ grinder go?" asked Sarah.

"Oh Sarah, you don't know how much pleasure it gives me to hear your cynical wit return."

"Does it mean we'd be giving up a lot?"

"I don't think so, Sarah. We can't be certain about it. But it would be tricky to prove the individuals are liable. We'd have to pierce the corporate veil, as lawyers say. We might never get there."

"It's a good deal, then?"

"It's a good deal. We shut the organization down. We get a lot of cash. We have some decisions to make about the terms for how we get to manage the cash. I want to wrap the BLM board into that discussion. I'll meet with them tomorrow and I want you to be there too."

Alicia could only imagine the conversations between Gerald Croome and the folks who made the decisions at Second Amendment. Sarah's question was a good one: Why would they agree?

There were, she supposed, individuals who had moved money in and out of Second Amendment's coffers, and who now might be vulnerable to personal liability for a huge punitive damages award if the case went to trial and verdict. They would not have insurance to protect them from a punitive damages award. They faced, perhaps, the risk of losing their houses, their possessions, of being forced into bankruptcy, of public shame.

And so, the lawyers, with periodic consultations with their respective clients, negotiated the complex terms of a settlement, memorialized in a formal agreement. In a memo to her clients— Sarah, Manny, Tad, and the BLM board—Alicia laid it out in plainer English.

It started with the preeminent fact that the court would enter a judgment in favor of the plaintiffs against Second Amendment, Inc. in the amount of $2.5 million. Then there were key provisions dealing with the management and distribution of the *known* funds, which didn't come close to the $2.5 million mark. Those funds, including the Second Amendment securities account, were to be transferred immediately into an escrow account temporarily managed by Shelby & Croome.

From the escrow account, the settlement called for several payments to be made by May 10, 2019: $150,000 to Green Mountain Black Lives Matter; $200,000 to Sarah Jacobson; $25,000 to Manny Cruz; and $5,000 to Tadeusz Sorowski. "I will not take more," he had said.

The sum of $60,000 would be retained in the Croome Escrow Account only as necessary to wind down the operations of Second Amendment and to comply with the remaining terms of the settlement and any further orders of the court. Otherwise, Second Amendment was required to cease all operations immediately.

All disbursements and transactions respecting the Croome Escrow Account were to be reported to Alicia Santana and were subject to review by the court upon request.

Of even greater interest to the plaintiffs, the terms of settlement required that the *balance* of Second Amendment's currently disclosed assets (approximately $490,000) be transferred by May 10 into a different escrow account, this one managed by Jacobson & Santana. And any funds remaining in the Croome Escrow Account after the winding-down process was concluded would also be transferred to the Santana Escrow Account.

The red meat of the settlement concerned the disposition of the Santana Escrow Account. Alicia had sole discretion to make payments from that account, over the ensuing five years, to non-profit organizations engaged in racial justice work, which may include but were not limited to Green Mountain BLM.

Next came provisions to deal with the unknown. To attempt to recover the balance of its $2.5 million judgment, the plaintiffs were permitted to pursue post-judgment discovery to determine if Second Amendment had other assets not hitherto disclosed, or if there were affiliated organizations or persons to whom it had fraudulently transferred funds without full consideration. Second Amendment and its principal officers were required to cooperate with these discovery efforts, at the risk of facing contempt-of-court penalties. Any additional funds that might be recovered would be added to the Santana Escrow Account.

A portion of the escrowed funds would be allocated to reimbursement of the plaintiffs' legal fees and expenses. Technical provisions of the agreement required Alicia to provide prompt notice to Gerald Croome of proposed distributions for this purpose, allowed Croome to file objections within a short time window, and retained jurisdiction in the court to adjudicate any such disputes or deal with any other matters that might arise under the terms of settlement.

And, in consideration of all of that, the plaintiffs would release all individuals associated with Second Amendment, Inc. from any and all civil claims, damages, and liabilities, aside from potential fraudulent transfer claims. The release explicitly did not apply to any criminal prosecutions the relevant prosecuting authorities may elect to pursue.

The settlement agreement and stipulation to judgment were promptly filed in court. Judge Wallis scheduled a hearing and directed the individual plaintiffs, not only the attorneys, to attend. They all appeared on the appointed day.

The courtroom was crowded with the press, movement members, and onlookers. Judge Wallis heard from the lawyers first. She then directed an inquiry from the bench. "Mr. Cruz?"

"Yes, your honor, I'm Manuel Cruz."

"Would you please stand?

"Oh. Yes."

"Have you reached the age of majority?"

"What?"

"How old are you now?"

"I'm eighteen."

"Thank you. Have you discussed the terms of the settlement with your lawyer, Ms. Santana?"

"Yes."

"Do you agree with the terms?"

"The way we're settling it? Yes, I do. For sure."

"Do you understand, Mr. Cruz, that you will be paid a total amount of $25,000, even though a great deal more money is being recovered from the defendant?"

"Yeah, I get that, your honor. I understand."

"And you understand it is possible that more assets will be located over time, but your own personal recovery will still be capped at $25,000. You understand that?"

"Yes, I understand."

"Do you think that's fair?"

Manny looked around. He saw his parents behind him. He looked at Sarah, who returned his gaze, and he took courage from her. "Fair? Yeah, I really do."

"Can you explain to me why you believe it is a fair settlement, a fair distribution of the funds recovered from Second Amendment, Inc.?"

"You've got to understand, Ma'am, most of the money is going to support Green Mountain BLM and other groups doing this kind of work. That's what I care about. The money coming to me? That's great and all. I need it for college. But look, what happened to me? I just got a racist email from these guys, calling me a spic. That's it. So twenty-five grand is generous, okay? Sarah? She deserves a lot more for what happened to her. Way more. I can't even imagine."

Here, Manny paused to look around again. "I can't even imagine," he repeated. "But mostly, what I want is to continue the struggle. We got fascism here. We got this president, I don't know how you feel, your honor Judge, but he's a fascist and a racist. He hates people like me, Americans like me. It's not just him either. He's got the whole Republican party tagging along and then millions of supporters lapping it all up."

Manny stayed standing and waited a moment. The judge did not interrupt. She nodded, giving him permission to continue. "They put my brothers and sisters in cages on the border. They divide us up. We're not white people, so we don't count. We're from shithole countries. I'm sorry to use that language, but it's the language of the president. I don't know, your honor Judge. I'm scared for my family. I'm scared for this country."

Again he paused, and a large number of those attending the hearing clapped.

"All right," said the judge. The clapping subsided, and she said, "Thank you, Mr. Cruz."

"Oh, and I got to say this too. We can't get away from all the cops killing Black people. That's what Black Lives Matter comes from. Like Eric Garner? You know who he is, right, your honor? He was the Black man choked to death by the white cop in Staten Island because he was selling cigarettes on the street. And it's just in the news now that they're not going to bring charges against the white cop whose arms were around his throat.

"Why not? He couldn't breathe. He kept telling the cops he couldn't breathe. Over and over. He was killed five years ago. You must have seen that, Judge. And the white cop, I forget his name, he just kept choking Eric Garner. That's whose name I remember, Judge. Eric Garner. He's not the only one either. There're lots more, Blacks and people of color killed by police when they shouldn't be, when they've done nothing wrong, or just something small wrong, like, you know, selling cigarettes or whatever.

"Cops sometimes kill white people too, sure, but not in the same numbers. I bet it's going to keep happening. It might be New York one month, or Ferguson another month, then another city here, another there. We have less value than whites. I don't mean I believe that, just so you understand. I mean we're *given* less value. We're not treated the same. It's like our bodies don't belong to us. That's why we've got to keep saying Black lives matter.

"So, I'm sorry, Judge, for going on and on. This settlement? It's fair the way the money goes. We're supposed to stand up for the rights of everyone. And I'm pretty much a kid. It shouldn't be my burden, you know? We've got to do everything we can to stop this."

Manny sat. The clapping was louder this time. Judge Wallis let it come to a natural close. She said, "I remember who Eric Garner is, Mr. Cruz. Thank you for your statement. Ms. Jacobson? Do you believe this settlement is fair to you?"

Sarah took her turn standing. "Yes, your honor, I do. Manny said it all better than I could have."

"You heard my questions to Mr. Cruz about the payments to the individual plaintiffs being capped?"

"Yes, and I understand all that. I approve of the terms."

"And are you satisfied with the arrangement providing for Attorney Santana, or her designee if she chooses, to exercise sole discretion over the disposition of the largest part of the recovered funds?"

"We talked a lot about that. Yes, that makes sense to me."

"Very well. Is there anything else you wish to tell the court?"

"I'm just relieved it's over. Thank you, your honor."

"All right. I'm very sorry for the terrible hardship you went through, Ms. Jacobson. I do hope you are healing from your ordeal."

"Thank you, your honor, I am. May I add one point?" The judge nodded. "In addition to how the funds are to be distributed—that's important, but in addition to that—what's critical for me is that we stopped this organization from continuing to harass and threaten and harm people who are seeking racial justice. We stopped them."

Clapping again. "All right," said the judge. "And can you also tell me whether the organization, Green Mountain Black Lives Matter, consents to the terms of the settlement?"

"Yes, they do."

Alicia stood and spoke. "Your honor, we submitted a signed board resolution to that effect. The chairman of the organization's board, Chip Skinner, is seated over here"—she motioned to her left—"and can address the court if you wish."

"Thank you, Ms. Santana. How do you do, Mr. Skinner."

Skinner stood. "Very well, thank you. And you?"

"Fine," said the judge. "Do you have any questions or concerns about the settlement terms?"

"No, I do not, your honor," replied Skinner. "We considered it all thoroughly. I can tell you every member of our board, all of whom are present in this courtroom, endorse this settlement agreement."

"Very well. Mr. Sorowski, do you also agree the settlement is fair?"

"Yes, your honor, I believe it is a fair settlement."

"Same questions regarding the caps on individual recovery and the discretion vested in Ms. Santana?"

"I agree with all aspects of the settlement, your honor."

"Thank you. I hope I will soon see you back before me as an attorney, not a party to litigation."

"Thank you, your honor. I hope that will be so, as well."

"Mr. Croome," asked the judge, "are you able to represent that you have consulted with the Second Amendment Board of Directors, that they understand the terms of this settlement, and that they consent to the terms?"

"Yes, your honor. Well, that is almost the case. I have consulted with the Chairman of the Board, Dmitri Rastapopolous, and with the executive director, Neil Davison, and they have assured me that is the case. You will see that Mr. Rastapopolous has signed the agreement as duly authorized agent of the non-profit corporation."

"His name's Rastapopolous?"

"Yes, your honor."

"All right." The judge paused and leaned forward. "I find that the terms of the settlement have been entered into knowledgably and voluntarily by the parties. I make this finding on the record in view of the fact that a substantial portion of the monetary recovery in this case is being paid not directly to the plaintiffs themselves, but is instead being delivered to the plaintiffs' attorney in escrow for eventual distribution to non-profit organizations at her discretion. At her sole discretion.

"Everyone understands that and approves. The court will issue both the stipulated judgment and the settlement agreement as orders of the court, and will retain jurisdiction as described and for the reasons set forth in the settlement agreement."

The judge removed her glasses. "I thank the parties and attorneys for their work in resolving the matter before the court. Are there any further matters to take up at this time?"

There were none.

The gavel banged. They stood.

Eventually, in another courtroom, Neil Davison, Keith Thomas, and Kyle Thomas, with his right arm in a sling, would plead guilty to criminal counts of kidnapping and conspiracy. All three would go to prison. The evidence against Marty Frazier was insufficient, the prosecutors concluded, to support those charges. Separately, he entered a plea to criminally threatening Sarah, Tad, and Manny. He got off on two years' probation, no prison time. Collin Chapman, the U-32 high school student, remained an angry young man.

Sarah took an unpaid leave of absence from work. She was greatly distracted, occasionally beset by bouts of fear and flashbacks that stopped her in her tracks, unsolicited moments of searing memories of her captivity. The man in the Trump mask stood at the doorway looking in at her. He haunted her.

Ricky's approach was to keep talking about it. "What are you feeling today?" "Tell me more about what you remember." "Don't keep it all inside, Sarah." "How did you deal with your loneliness in the cell?" "I am always here for you." "I'm ready to listen now if you will talk to me." "You want to write a journal?" "Please, sweetie."

He didn't really know what he was doing. He wasn't following a guidebook or a therapist's advice. He was just speaking from the heart, as he always did.

Sarah could not respond in kind. She couldn't verbalize most of her experience because she couldn't rationalize it. Her fear was not translatable into language. She grew numb and unresponsive.

This went on for many days. Ricky suffered. Then came a warm spring day when she returned home in the early afternoon from a walk—she took many walks—and said to Ricky, "I'm sorry, my sweet Ricky. You are unbelievably patient."

Ricky was at the kitchen table, studying lesson plans for the coming days so he could appropriately tailor his tutoring duties. "Oh, Sarah," he stammered. "Nothing to be sorry about." He considered. "To be sorry to me about."

"Can we go out in the canoe, do you think?" she asked.

They shared a canoe with Sarah's parents. They put the rack on the roof of the Civic, drove up to Adams Street, put the canoe on the roof rack and the paddles and life vests in the back seat with the towels, and drove the short distance to the reservoir. It was late May, the water still bitter cold, the crabapples blossoming everywhere.

They put in at the boat launch and paddled north up the lake to where the beaver and heron made their homes. They were the only ones on the water. The warm sunlight bathed them from the west, bouncing reflections of the water into the woods and brush on the east bank.

Ricky, in the stern, watched Sarah paddling, as he feathered his stroke and guided the canoe to follow the contours of the bank. Her dark hair was short and a bit spiky. She had removed her fleece and he admired her strong, bare arms and her back. He felt joy in being present with her in this canoe in this lake at this moment and wanted to be with her at all moments.

She placed her paddle down and turned to look at him. They floated forward.

A little farther on, the lake opened and became very shallow, and the banks here were muddy, with beaver paths visible in the brush. Their paddles bumped the bottom, disturbing the silt.

Then the reservoir narrowed and deepened and became a slow brook that curved between the rocks and the bright green vegetation spilling over the banks.

They pulled up at a smooth ledge of rock, tying the canoe to a sapling. They put the towels down on the rock. A blue heron flapped slowly toward them and landed in the rushes across the brook.

Feeling the mood was right and the time was ripe, Ricky began to make love to Sarah. But he had misunderstood, and the truth was more complicated. Sarah put her hands on his chest and pushed him back, said, "I can't," and pulled her fleece on.

When Ricky looked into her eyes, they were dark and reflected nothing back.

"No?" he asked.

"I imagine," she said, "there is a man who smells like creosote looking in at me around a shower curtain. I'm sorry, Ricky."

Ricky held her hand and waited. Then he asked, "You did say he left you alone in the shower, right?"

"Yes, yes, yes. I think he did that, in a way. I told you already. But you've got to understand. He had all the power. It was all up to him, not up to me."

The brook flowed slowly by, the water glittering and occasionally slapping the ledge. The heron mysteriously remained in place on the other side, unmoving.

"I feel like I'm becoming crazy," Sarah said.

"No."

"You don't want this—why should you?" Sarah looked down and didn't meet his eyes. "You can move on, Ricky."

"Sarah, come on. It's not a matter of what I want. You are my partner. I'm with you. I'm staying with you."

"Yeah, you can say that now. What if I stay like this, a frightened porcupine? How long will your patience last?" Sarah now looked up at him.

His eyes were tearing.

"Ricky, you remember I've talked about Tyrene?"

"Sure. Tyrene."

"I abandoned him, you know. Because he was crazy, he was bipolar. I couldn't handle that. He was in such pain, Ricky, and I couldn't meet him where he was. I let him drown. I said I loved him, but my love wasn't deep enough."

Ricky wanted to contradict her. He was about to speak, but something in her face stopped him, and he realized this time it was best not to argue with her, but to wait and listen, and to keep holding her hand in his.

The heron lifted its wings and slowly rose up and flew away. Both of them watched the heron.

"What are you saying?" he finally asked.

"I don't know," she said. She was facing back up the brook where the heron had disappeared. "What if that happens to me?"

Ricky just looked at her in astonishment.

Sarah continued, "Tyrene told me once that he landed in the wrong place in life. His words. I think I understand now. I have landed in the wrong place in life. What if I can't escape it?"

Ricky put his hands on her cheeks and cradled her head with his long fingers. He said, "Being with you, Sarah, is the right place in life for me."

A breeze picked up and the cold of the rock made them shiver. They put their stuff back in the canoe and paddled back to where the reservoir opened up.

"I'll keep paddling with you," Ricky said to Sarah's back.

About the Author

B ernie Lambek practices law in Montpelier, Vermont. His first novel, *Uncivil Liberties*, was published by Rootstock Publishing in 2018.

Also avaiable from Rootstock Publishing

The Atomic Bomb on My Back
Taniguchi Sumiteru

Blue Desert
Celia Jeffries

*China in Another Time: A
Personal Story*
Claire Malcolm Lintilhac

An Everyday Cult
Gerette Buglion

*Fly with A Murder of Crows:
A Memoir*
Tuvia Feldman

Horodno Burning: A Novel
Michael Freed-Thall

The Inland Sea: A Mystery
Sam Clark

Junkyard at No Town
J.C. Myers

*The Language of Liberty:
A Citizen's Vocabulary*
Edwin C. Hagenstein

A Lawyer's Life to Live
Kimberly B. Cheney

Lifting Stones: Poems
Doug Stanfield

The Lost Grip: Poems
Eva Zimet

Lucy Dancer
Story and Illustrations by Eva Zimet

Nobody Hitchhikes Anymore
Ed Griffin-Nolan

*Preaching Happiness: Creating a Just
and Joyful World*
Ginny Sassaman

*Red Scare in the Green Mountains: Ver-
mont in the McCarthy Era 1946-1960*
Rick Winston

Safe as Lightning: Poems
Scudder H. Parker

Street of Storytellers
Doug Wilhelm

*Tales of Bialystok: A Jewish Journey
from Czarist Russia to America*
Charles Zachariah Goldberg

To the Man in the Red Suit: Poems
Christina Fulton

Uncivil Liberties: A Novel
Bernie Lambek

Venice Beach: A Novel
William Mark Habeeb

The Violin Family
Melissa Perley; Illustrated by
Fiona Lee Maclean

Walking Home: Trail Stories
Celia Ryker

Wave of the Day: Collected Poems
Mary Elizabeth Winn

*Whole Worlds Could Pass Away:
Collected Stories*
Rickey Gard Diamond

*You Have a Hammer: Building Grant
Proposals for Social Change*
Barbara Floersch